STRANGER AT
THE DOOR

by

MAY COATES

HARLEQUIN BOOKS

TORONTO
WINNIPEG

Original hard cover edition published in 1971
by Mills & Boon Limited, 17-19 Foley Street,
London W1A 1DR, England

© May Coates 1971

SBN 373-01677-8

Harlequin edition published April 1973

The Harlequin trade mark, consisting of the word
HARLEQUIN and the portrayal of a Harlequin, is registered
in the United States Patent Office and in the Canada Trade
Marks Office.

Printed in Canada

1677

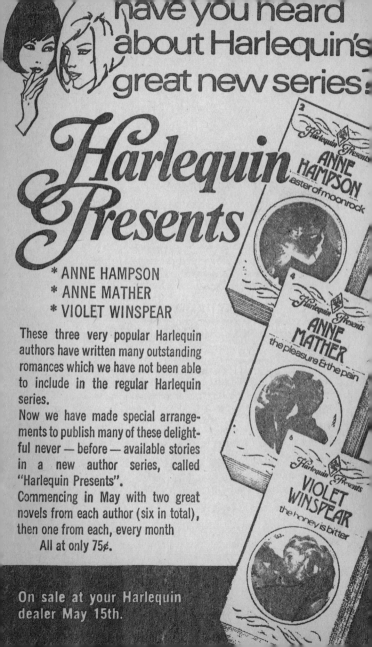

WELCOME

TO THE WONDERFUL WORLD

of Harlequin Romances!

Interesting, informative and entertaining,
each Harlequin Romance portrays an appealing
love story. Harlequin Romances take you
to faraway places — places with real people
facing real love situations — and
you become part of their story.

As publishers of Harlequin Romances, we're extremely
proud of our books (we've been publishing
them since 1954). We're proud also that Harlequin
Romances are North America's most-read
paperback romances.

Eight new titles are released every month and are
sold at nearly all book-selling stores across
Canada and the United States.

A free catalogue listing all available Harlequin Romances
can be yours by writing to the

HARLEQUIN READER SERVICE,
M.P.O. Box 707, Niagara Falls, N.Y. 14302.
Canadian address: Stratford, Ontario, Canada.

or use order coupon at back of book.

We sincerely hope you enjoy reading
this Harlequin Romance.

Yours truly,

THE PUBLISHERS
  Harlequin Romances

For George and Nora

CHAPTER I

'There's the taxi now.' Mr Everard turned back into the Salon. He had been looking out over the balcony, down on to the Quai de Mont Blanc.

Verity came to stand beside him. She stared across the lake, hoping perhaps for one last glimpse of Mont Blanc, but the clouds hung low and veiled the majestic peak.

'I'm sorry to hurry you, but we'll have to go.' The kindly, elderly man guided her back into the room and rang the bell for the concierge. Verity's two suitcases were standing on the shiny parquet floor of the hall. As Pierre took the bags and Mr Everard held the door open, her eyes misted as, with one final look, she said goodbye to the kind of life she had led for the past five years.

The lift bore them swiftly down to the ground floor and they came out into the street. It was July and workmen were hanging flowers, flags, bunting and fairy lights ready for the Fête de Genève. *Le jet d'eau* sprang from the centre of the lake, its torrent of rainbow spray sparkling in the sunlight. The *mouettes* sped back and forth across the water and the pleasure steamer hooted as it left the quay.

It was a long ride to the airport, and from the moment they arrived at the busy, crowded place, Verity felt an intense feeling of excitement. She sensed that Mr Everard was obviously anxious to do his best for her and see her safely on her journey to England, but she knew he had an urgent appointment, from the way he constantly glanced at his watch.

' I can manage quite well now.' Verity spoke with more confidence than she actually felt.

' I can spare a few more minutes, Verity. You understand the position when you get to London?'

' Yes, I have the letter.' She fumbled in her hand-bag.

'*I shall be at London Airport to meet you—*' She read the words and, raising her eyes from the page, she said softly, ' —and it's signed Father.'

Mr Everard felt a sudden twinge of compassion for the girl.

' I do wish,' he said, ' that your—' he stumbled over the words—' your guardian—had told you the truth about your real parents.'

' Poor Daddy! You know,' she said in a sudden rush of emotion, ' I don't think I shall ever be able to think of him as my guardian, but—' and her face lit up, ' isn't it wonderful, Mr Everard, to be going to meet a whole new family? Do you think they'll like me?'

Mr Everard coughed and blew his nose loudly.

' I don't see how anyone could help liking you. The letter shows that they are ready to accept you, but—' and he paused, seeking for the right words. ' I'm sure that after the first strangeness has worn off you are going to be very happy at Mardale. As soon as the property here is sold I will let you know the position about your money. I fear that there won't be much—such a pity Mr Blanchard dipped into his capital.'

' I shall get a job.' Her chin tilted and her soft lips took on a firm line.

He sighed. ' It might be a good idea to use some of your small capital to train for a post. After all, twenty is not very old, you have plenty of time. I

8

don't know what your father's position is now, but he has a family and his business is not a large one.

'Now, my dear, I shall have to leave you.' He beckoned to a porter and gave instructions. 'The flight is due to leave in half an hour and, remember, when you get to London don't leave the airport until your father arrives. Wait in the lounge and he will easily find you, and—' he took her hand '—I am always available if you need advice. Write to us, but I shall be in London in a month and will arrange a meeting.'

'Goodbye, dear Mr Everard. I don't know what I should have done without you and, of course, your wife. I shall always remember all you've done for me,' and she stood on tiptoe and kissed his cheek.

As the porter guided the girl to the departure lounge, Mr Everard hurried away, turning once to wave, but with his mind obviously already on the important appointment he had mentioned.

The flight to England was not eventful. Verity had flown before to many parts of the world with her guardian, who had been in the Diplomatic Service. She scarcely glanced out of the window as the plane took off. Although she had been happy in Geneva, now she was looking forward with an intensity of longing to meeting her real father. It had been a blow, after the death of the man who had been so dear and kind, to find out from Mr Everard that she had not even been related to him in any way. Mr Everard had explained it all, how he had often advised Guy Blanchard to tell Verity the true facts, but how Guy Blanchard had not listened. Instead, Guy had left a letter of instructions to Mr Everard, and another to Verity's father, which had been dispatched immediately after the funeral.

9

Verity felt that she could hardly wait. Treated as a beloved only daughter by Guy Blanchard and his wife, she had sometimes longed for sisters and brothers, and now she was to become part of a whole new family. Mr Everard had been hazy about the matter, but he had said that John Gardner had several other children. Verity's mother had died at her birth and Guy and Rosa, his wife, had offered to take the baby. They had lost their own small daughter only a few months earlier. They had wanted to adopt Verity legally, but her father stubbornly refused to allow them to do so and, fearing that he would demand the child's return, they had let the matter drop. It was four years later that he married for the second time and so somehow, although he had always intended to have Verity back some day, the years had passed, he had more children and now Verity was a young woman of twenty, and a stranger.

Rosa Blanchard had died when Verity was seventeen and since then she had lived in Geneva with the man she thought of as her father. His health had become precarious and Verity, although so young, had nursed him devotedly until four weeks ago he had died.

The great jet ate up the miles and it seemed a very short time before the passengers were told to fasten their safety belts. It was hazy over London Airport —one of those dull, muggy summer days, but Verity felt no pang of longing for the brilliant blue skies of Geneva.

She was still buoyed up by this almost suffocating sensation of excitement, which had come when she had apparently been left entirely alone in the world and then discovered that she was part of a family.

Although her grief at the loss of Guy Blanchard was very poignant still, she could hardly restrain her impatience for the moment, half dreaded, when she would meet her father.

It seemed an eternity before she was through the Customs, and then, as she seated herself in the lounge, an announcement came over the loudspeaker.

' *Will Miss Verity Blanchard go to the nearest information desk, please?*'

The cool voice of the girl at the desk asked,

' Miss Verity Blanchard?'

' Yes.'

' There is a message for you, Miss Blanchard. Mr Gardner is unable to be at the airport to meet you. Will you make your way to the restaurant where Dr Rhodes will call for you at three-thirty.'

Making sure that her bags were safe in the left luggage office, she picked up her light travelling-case and slowly climbed the stairs to the airy restaurant. It seemed that she was expected, as the head waiter came forward, and, after asking her name, led her to table near the large windows which looked out over the runway. She had lunched on the plane and did not feel inclined for more food, but she ordered a pot of coffee. She glanced at her watch. The time was only two-thirty which meant another hour to wait in suspense. Her father must have had some other important engagement, she mused, and wondered about Dr Rhodes.

The time passed slowly and she watched the planes arrive and depart; people kept coming and going until at last she noticed the arrival of a tall dark man. He was looking round the dining room as if searching for someone, and then, as he spoke to the waiter and turned to look in her direction, her heart began to pound as she realised that this must be her father's deputy. As he strode across to her table, she half rose from her seat. She got an impression of a stern, somewhat forbidding face. As Verity got to her feet, he motioned her to sit down and took the chair opposite.

'Miss Blanchard? I'm sorry I'm a little late,' he said. 'Let me introduce myself. I'm Dr Garnett Rhodes. Now, I'll order lunch.'

'Not for me, please. I had a meal on the plane.'

'You won't mind if I have mine? I've been attending a conference and I was delayed by the heavy traffic in getting out of the city.

'You'll be wondering,' he said at last when the waiter had taken his order, 'why I'm here to meet you instead of Mr John Gardner. He's had to go into hospital and may be there for some weeks. He might have to have an operation, but until further tests have been done we shan't know. In any event he'll have to take things quietly for a few months.

'Have you met Mr Gardner before, Miss Blanchard?' he continued, as she did not speak.

She thought that she detected a note of impatience in his voice. 'No, I haven't met him,' she said quietly.

'Everything happened so suddenly that his wife was not aware that you were coming until she was going through the papers on his desk. She found the letter from Mr Everard giving the day and time of your arrival.'

'Then she's expecting me?' Verity leaned forward eagerly.

'I think it only fair to tell you that although Mrs Gardner is the most generous and warm-hearted person, your arrival is bound to cause her a little inconvenience. She has not only her own two children but also her husband's family by his first marriage. However,' he continued more kindly, ' it would no doubt be a help if you could cut your stay as short as possible. Now,' he glanced at his watch and summoned the waiter, ' I must take you to the hotel. I've booked you in at a very comfortable place. I myself am staying with a friend. I have to attend a reception tonight, so we can't travel to Yorkshire until tomorrow.'

As if in a dream, Verity gathered up her things and as they came down the steps from the restaurant she told him that some of her luggage was to be collected. There was a question she must ask, but this did not seem to be the time for it. She felt sick with anxiety about her father. What if things were more serious than Dr Rhodes had told her? She was quiet as they drove away from the airport.

Garnett Rhodes drove into the hotel garage and, as Verity's luggage was carried upstairs and she signed the visitors' book, she saw him turn sharply as someone tapped him on the shoulder.

' I though you were attending some dreary medical conference,' said the newcomer lightheartedly. The good-looking young man accompanied the words with a knowing wink. ' Aren't you going to introduce me?' The young man's glance at Verity was frankly admiring.

' Mr Gerard Manley, Miss Verity Blanchard.' Dr Rhodes sounded stiff and unfriendly as he made the introduction.

' I'm booking Miss Blanchard in here for the night. Unfortunately I shall have to leave her this evening as I'm bound to attend the reception at the Grand.'

' And you can't disappoint Margot either!' There

seemed to be a faint touch of malice in the remark and the dark eyes of the doctor became even more clouded as he frowned, and then, to Verity, he said:

'I'm sorry about this, but I'm sure you'll be quite all right here, and I'll call for you at nine-thirty tomorrow morning.'

Gerard Manley did not seem impressed. 'Rubbish, Garnett, that's no way for any girl to spend an evening in London. Luckily,' and he gave an impish smile, 'I have two tickets for a musical and I should be delighted to look after Miss Blanchard for you.'

Dr Rhodes seemed as if he were going to object to this suggestion when Verity, who had been standing there feeling a strong desire to get to her room and burst into tears, suddenly took a hand in the proceedings. She smiled up at Gerard Manley and both men were startled as the small oval face became illuminated, two deep dimples creased her cheeks and the hazel eyes blazed provocatively before she spoke.

'That would be lovely, thank you, Mr Manley. You're very kind. What time shall I be ready?'

'Where are you staying?' Dr Rhodes asked Gerard Manley abruptly.

'Not here.' The impish look came again. 'I'm staying with my sister Monica. I called to book a room for my mother who is coming up next week. She prefers to be quiet, and Monica's brood are not exactly restful.'

'That's settled then, thank you, Dr Rhodes. There's no need to worry about me. I'll be ready in good time tomorrow.'

He hesitated and then with a curt nod to them both went out through the swing doors of the hotel.

'I say,' said Gerard sympathetically, 'you look tired out. Come into the lounge and I'll order tea.'

Taking her arm, he piloted her across to the lounge. It was an old-fashioned but peaceful room. A number of elderly people were sitting at small tables and he took her across to the settee by the open window. Soon she was sipping tea and listening to the gay flow of trivial conversation. It gave her a little longer time before she must face the fact that no one seemed to know about her. It seemed strange that her father, who had written the affectionate letter tucked away in her handbag, had evidently not even told his wife the truth about her.

With a start, she realised that Gerard had asked a question.

' Do forgive me,' she said. ' I was thinking about Mr Gardner. I'm on my way to Mardale to meet him and I had so little time to find out whether his illness is serious or not. He should have met me at the airport.'

' I don't think you would get much information out of Dr Rhodes, but then Mr Gardner is his senior partner's patient and I suppose it wouldn't be etiquette to talk about it. Cheer up,' he continued. ' I think it's some flare-up of an old trouble which he's neglected for a long time. He's in very good hands, and he's a tough, wiry man.'

She smiled gratefully. The little interlude had done her good and her spirits rose. She probably was worrying unnecessarily, she thought, and it was possible that Mrs Gardner had not had time to tell the doctor about her.

' I'll have to go now, but be ready at six-thirty. We can have a light meal and then perhaps go on for supper after the show.'

' I'll stay here for a little while,' she answered. ' There's plenty of time before I need to change.'

With a gay salute he left her and Verity sat for another half hour, lost in thought, oblivious of the glances cast by some of the elderly ladies at the other end of the room.

Gerard Manley drew a sharp breath as Verity came down the hotel stairs into the rather sombre entrance that evening. Her shining, honey-coloured hair was now piled high. Her simple dress was white, and over her arm she carried a mink stole. She wore a double string of pearls and matching earrings. Verity herself felt a sensation of pleasure as she joined the young man. Gerard's good looks and gay demeanour gave the promise of a happy evening in the city, which temporarily at least would help her to forget her problems.

She was not to be disappointed. Tired but happy, much later that night she came back to the hotel, having learned a lot about Mardale. Gerard had been able to tell her many things she had longed to know. She knew now that she had an elder brother, John, twenty-five years old and married; a sister, Sara, twenty-three, a State registered nurse, and that also she had a stepbrother and a stepsister. She had listened intently and at times she had wondered if Gerard thought it strange that she should know so little about the family she was to visit.

After he had left her, Verity slept soundly so that when the maid drew the curtains she sat up unable for a moment to realise that she was in a strange place. By the time Garnett Rhodes arrived she was ready, her suitcases waiting by the desk. He was in a hurry and after a brief greeting they went out to the car.

' I hope Manley looked after you,' Garnett said in

his usual clipped way.

'He was very kind and thoughtful,' she said softly. 'I loved the musical, and supper afterwards at Quaglino's.'

'Your first visit to London?'

'Oh no, I've been many times before, but most of my life has been spent abroad.' She hesitated for a minute before she continued. 'I've lived for the last five years in Geneva because of my—' In spite of herself, her voice trembled and her companion said,

'I understand that you've recently lost your—'

'Yes,' she interrupted, not wishing to go into further details with this dark, abrupt man. She could not help thinking of the gay, friendly Gerard Manley who had for a few hours made her feel happy. He had been attentive to every wish and she was glad that he too lived in Mardale.

'I suppose Mr Blanchard was a great friend of John Gardner?'

'They had known each other for many years; were at school and University together. It's a pity that you were not told of his illness before you left Geneva.'

'I suppose you mean, Dr Rhodes, that my presence is going to be an inconvenience to the family?'

'You must admit,' he spoke sharply again, 'it's not exactly the best of times for them to have to entertain a guest.'

She was silent for so long that he stopped the car and turned to her.

'I'm sorry, I shouldn't have said that. It's just that it seemed that Mary had enough to contend with at the moment and—'

'Dr Rhodes!' The hazel eyes blazed once more,

but with anger this time. 'If you'll stop at the next town I can take the next train back to London and stay in a hotel until Mr Everard has settled my affairs.'

'How old are you?'

'Twenty.'

'Look.' He put his large brown hand over hers and in spite of the dislike he had aroused in her she felt the warmth of his grasp and her sudden spurt of defiance died as she tried to keep her tears from spilling over. 'I'm sorry, I'd no right to lecture you. Of course you must come to Mardale as arranged. I'm an interfering busybody.' He smiled almost for the first time since she first saw him and his penetrating light grey eyes were smiling too.

He started up the car again and she regained her composure, and when they stopped for lunch she was able to talk. They did not touch on her private affairs, but he found that she was a surprisingly good conversationalist. Her training in acting as hostess for her guardian stood her in good stead and he was almost sorry when they were on the road once more. He wanted to be in Mardale as early as possible and so was glad that she was silent now and that he could concentrate on the road.

It was not until they were threading their way through the congestion of traffic in Leeds that Verity began to realise that she was now in the heart of the West Riding of Yorkshire. She had never been so far north and her first glimpse of the dark buildings was not prepossessing. It was raining slightly and, although it was the month of June, the skies were overcast and unfriendly to her gaze. Coming from the brilliant Swiss sunshine it added to the depression she had felt ever since she knew that her father was ill. How long, she wondered, would it be before she could meet him?

In his turn, Garnett Rhodes wondered how this girl, obviously wealthy, with her background of world travel and knowledge of affairs, would fit into the happy-go-lucky household at Mardale. He knew the family well and had always enjoyed visiting them in the big, untidy family house on the outskirts of the little town. It was situated between Leeds and Harrogate and the family business was in the outskirts of Leeds.

'How far is it now?' The rather deep soft voice broke into his thoughts.

'About five miles.'

'Is there a telephone box near?'

'You can telephone from the house when we arrive.'

'I'd rather do it before we reach the house.'

He pulled into a layby and stopped the car. ' Any time during the last four hours you could have asked me to stop. Surely it can wait for another half-hour?'

'I'd rather telephone now,' she said firmly. 'As a matter of fact, I'm going to telephone to Beech House to find out if Mrs Gardner would rather I returned to London until this crisis is over.'

He felt a strong desire to shake her, but started the car once more and drove on. He pulled up again outside the Post Office and, before he could get out, she was in the telephone box. She pulled out a letter from her handbag and glanced at it, then fumbled in her purse. He chuckled to himself as she came out and across the pavement.

'You'll need two-pence pieces,' he said, and handed her four. 'Do you know how to use the new boxes?'

Without deigning to reply, Verity went back and he saw her studying the directions.

She seemed to have succeeded in making the connection and to be listening intently. At last she came back to the car and her expression was radiant.

'You can drive me to Beech House now, Dr Rhodes. My—Mrs Gardner is anxious to see me.'

It was about twenty minutes later that they came to the house and Verity was unable to take in any impression of her surroundings. She was conscious of one thing only—the desire to meet her father. All the doubts and fears of the past weeks seemed to crowd on top of her and, as she stood on the steps and the doctor brought out her luggage from the boot, her face had grown pale, so that he looked at her with concern. Her poised, sophisticated veneer had gone and she looked little more than a schoolgirl, young and defenceless.

The door swung open and a slim, dark woman with a tired but smiling face ran down the steps and, in a moment, the girl felt the warmth of those welcoming arms which enfolded her.

'Come in, my darling child, you must be worn out. Garnett, we can't thank you enough for taking care of her.'

'I won't come in now, Mary,' he replied. 'How is John?'

Her face clouded slightly as she answered:

'He's a little better, thank you, Garnett, but we don't know the results of the tests yet.'

Suddenly Verity felt as if she would like to call him back, but she was led into the house. Verity clutched Mary Gardner's arm.

'Do you know about—?' She could not finish the

sentence, but the other woman understood.

'Your father has just told me, but we won't talk now.'

She led the way up the wide, shabbily carpeted staircase.

'This is your room,' she announced, as she opened the door and led Verity into the small bedroom. 'I do hope you'll be comfortable. I know you've been used to a different standard of living, but my dear, dear girl—' She smiled with the radiant warmth of welcome which so endeared her to most people. 'Come down when you're ready. The bathroom is across the landing. I want to have a talk before the children get in.'

It didn't take Verity long to change into a light cotton frock. She hurried because she was eager to have the promised talk.

Mary came out of the kitchen as Verity reached the bottom of the stairs.

'Come out on to the terrace,' she said, and led the way out through the French windows of the big sitting-room.

Verity's thoughts were concentrated on the desire for news of her father. Mary seemed to sense this and she started straight away to explain that John Gardner was likely to be in hospital for quite a time. It was hoped that an operation could be avoided, she said.

'He's a lot better now,' she told Verity. 'Even after these few days of rest. It's overwork mainly and worry about the factory. Of course, he wants to see you as soon as possible. It was only today when I told him that Garnett Rhodes was meeting you at the airport that he told me the truth about you.'

'I wonder why—'

'I think that your father was almost afraid to break the news to me, when he asked me to marry him, that he was the father of not two but three children. He had a very difficult time after your mother died, a succession of housekeepers, and Robert and Sara were running wild. It took me a long time to win their confidence and I think he felt that you were safe and happy and that it wouldn't be fair to the Blanchards to take you from them.'

'He refused to let them adopt me. Mr Everard told me.'

'Yes, it was too final a step and every year he promised himself that he would take a break and go to see you, but the Blanchards were continually on the move and he hasn't been able to leave the business for more than a short holiday for a long time. It will be easier now that Robert can relieve him a bit, but trade is so bad at the moment and the plant requires such a great deal of modernisation.'

'Do my—?' Again Verity could not complete the sentence.

'The younger children do, but Robert and Sara have no idea. Your father was anxious to tell them himself, but now I feel we must break the news as soon as possible. They'll all be here for dinner tonight. Robert is bringing his wife over from Carbridge and Sara is bringing her fiancé, Michael Rowe. She's a staff nurse at a hospital in Leeds and Michael is training to become a hospital secretary.' She answered the unspoken question on Verity's face. 'It will be a bit of an ordeal for you. Would you like me to tell them before you meet? I think myself that if I have a word with them as soon as they arrive, the ice will be broken. You mustn't worry. It may take a little time for them to become accustomed to the idea of another sister.'

' Whatever you think best.' Verity sounded discouraged. All her hopes and happiness at the thought of meeting her real family had now evaporated and for the first time she began to realise that there was to be no joyful welcome, that she would have to earn their liking. She could not burst into their midst and be accepted as one of the family until she had proved herself. She felt so ill-equipped for the task. Her life abroad and in such different surroudings had been no preparation for the sort of life she was now to lead.

Mary sensed the trend of her thoughts.

' Remember, Verity, I'm behind you. I must admit at first I was quite bewildered by the news, but now I've seen you I know that there's no need to worry. You're very like your mother and I can see by that determined little chin that you have a good deal of your father's fighting spirit. Have patience, Robert and Sara are fine young people. They'll understand, and I have no worries about my two scamps.'

It was just before eight o'clock that evening and Verity had unpacked and arranged her clothes in the wardrobe. Her large trunks would come later and as she looked round she wondered if all her possessions would not prove to be an embarrassment, She surveyed herself in the dressing table mirror. Leaning forward, she could see that her face wore a tense and anxious expression. She tried a smile, but this was so forced and artificial that she concentrated on making sure that she did not look too dressed up. It was obvious that her dress was expensive, although it was the plainest she had with her. She did so much want to make a good impression on this first evening with her family. With a sigh, she rose and went out of the bedroom on to the square landing.

She could hear the sound of voices—the deep sound of a man speaking and then a lighter soprano. She leaned over the banister rail and looked down to where Mary was greeting her stepchildren by the open door. After removing their coats, they disappeared into the sitting room. Verity wondered whether to wait until Mary fetched her, but then she decided to take a walk round the garden. They would be able to see her from the windows and anything was better than staying up there in suspense.

She ran silently down to the hall and had just reached the door when the babel of conversation in the sitting-room stopped for a minute and then out of the silence a girl's scornful voice said:

' Well, I think she has a nerve! '

There was a low sound of remonstrance from Mary and then a man's voice.

' I must say I'm inclined to agree with Sara. It's a bit much to have a thing like this sprung on us. I wonder why on earth Father didn't tell us himself? I always thought that the baby died when Mother did.'

' Why on earth does she want to turn up now? She's never bothered about us before. Oh, Mary, you'd make excuses for the devil! Just because she's graciously decided to pay us a visit won't change my opinion.'

' Be quiet, both of you! ' Mary's voice was angry now. ' Verity is your sister. I insist on her being made welcome in this house, and that's what your father wishes. He's in no condition to speak to you himself, but Verity is to be treated properly. That's

24

my last word about it!'

Verity stood with her hand on the door knob. Whatever else she had anticipated, it was not this kind of antagonism. Then, before she could move, Mary came out into the hall and without appearing to notice that Verity was unusually pale, she led her into the room.

'Come in and meet your family, my dear.' She flashed a warning glance at the four people who stood by the big window at the other end of the room.

They came forward quietly enough.

'This is Sara.'

Verity held out her hand which was grasped and relinquished quickly by the tall brown-haired girl.

'This is Sara's fiancé.'

Verity looked up at the round pleasant face of Michael Rowe and felt for the first time that someone at least had a little sympathy for her. He held her hand firmly as he murmured a greeting. Then the tall dark-haired young man came forward. He looked down at Verity with an enigmatic expression on his face. He was good-looking, with a forceful strongly-featured face and square determined chin, and he in turn introduced his wife, who was small and a little plump but with very merry eyes. Her name was Laura and they had been married earlier in the year.

The rather constrained silence which fell was suddenly broken as the door burst open, and everyone's eyes turned to look at the sturdy little boy who stood there.

'Aren't we ever going to eat, Mum?' he asked, and as everyone laughed, he was pushed from behind and a girl, a little older, came in sight. She had mousy brown hair and a pale triangular little face, but the boy was red-haired and freckled and his blue eyes were frank and friendly.

'Is this her?' It was the girl who spoke.

'This, my dear little mouse, is your new half-sister.' Robert ruffled the child's hair as he spoke.

'She doesn't look any different.' This was said in a disappointed tone by the girl.

Mary hastened to explain. 'They've both been so excited ever since I told them you were coming this morning. I don't know what they expected. These are my two, Dinah and Simon.'

'I thought you said she'd be horrible.' Simon stared accusingly at his sister.

'Oh well, she's a "step", isn't she?' And then the mischievous plain little face broke into a grin and a small hand crept into Verity's. 'I think you look quite nice anyway,' she announced, and then again Simon caused a diversion by asking in heartfelt tones,

'Aren't we ever going to eat?'

Mary led the way into the dining-room and, as the meal proceeded, Verity could not have told anyone about the food. The ball of conversation flashed from one to the other so rapidly that she was bewildered but even more fascinated as she tried to follow the conversation. This was really the first time in her life that she had been part of a family gathering.

For the most part, except for Mary and Michael Rowe addressing her, she would have taken little part in the talk. She began to feel desperately tired and it was with a feeling of thankfulness that she excused herself when Mary noticed how silent she had become, and remembered that it had been a long and tiring day for her. First there had been the journey from London, and then the meeting with the family.

The two children were also sent off to bed and accompanied Verity upstairs after she had said good-night to the others. The memory of that conversation she had heard still occupied Verity's thoughts, but when the two children seemed anxious to look into her room, she was glad of their company. At least they were genuine and surely would have no prejudices to overcome.

'We'd better go to bed,' Simon warned.

'Oh, all right then. I say!' Dinah bounced up and down on the bed. 'I think it's fun to have a stepsister.'

'You've always had a stepsister. Sara is one,' replied Simon stolidly.

'Oh, well, you know what I mean, I think it's fun. Wait until I tell the girls at school. It's like a story out of a book.' And then, with a rapid change of mood, 'I think you're nice, Verity, nicer than Sara. She's bad-tempered often.'

'Oh, come on, Dinah, you know Sara doesn't mean anything. She gets tired working at that hospital and doing all those exams. I like Robert and Sara.' Simon's blue eyes glared at his sister and then: 'I think you're nice too, Verity.'

And with this comforting remark he pulled his reluctant sister out of the bedroom.

Verity sat in the armchair by the window for a long time, too tired to get ready for bed. It had been such a confusing day and she was left with the unpalatable convinction that it was going to be a hard task to make herself a niche in the family circle. If only she could meet her father! It was curious, the feeling she had that once he came back her troubles would be lessened. She had not met him, had only the one letter he had written to her.

Verity felt the prickle of tears behind her eyes. It seemed such a long time since she had had any close contact with another woman. She had been happy with Guy Blanchard in their quiet years in Geneva after the death of his wife, but how she had longed for the friendship of someone of her own sex. As she had looked into the kind, soft eyes of her stepmother, who could understandably have resented her presence, she realised that here was someone prepared to love her as she had cared for and loved her other stepchildren. It did not matter that her clothes were not particularly smart, her hair unfashionably curly and streaked with grey.

Suddenly Verity felt she could think no more, and the lids closed over her hazel eyes and she selpt soundly on this first night in her new home.

CHAPTER II

Mary turned to give a reassuring smile at Verity as they went into the side entrance of the great hospital.

'I'll see what Sister says before we venture to let you in. I know he's longing for this moment just as eagerly as you are, but he's making such good progress now, we mustn't risk any upset.'

'I know,' Verity answered, 'but I don't think I can wait much longer.'

The lift took them up to the top floor. It was an enormous place. Porters, nurses and visitors all seemed to make the building teem with activity.

Sister came out from her office to answer their enquiries. She smiled at the two women. 'Mr Gardner is very much better today. Doctor Soames is delighted with his progress.'

'Do you think——?'

Sister understood what Mary meant. She had been told about Verity and it had been on her advice that they had waited for these few days before letting the girl meet her father.

'It will be quite in order for you to go in to see him today.' She smiled at them. 'Don't stay too long on this first visit, and I think Mrs Gardner had better go in first to let him know you're here.'

It seemed a long ten minutes as Verity chatted to the kindly, fresh-faced girl who seemed to be so young to be in charge of a large hospital ward. Then Mary reappeared, her face happier and less care-worn than it had been since Verity first met her.

'He's so much better, it's hardly believable. I'll take you in to him and then I'll leave you for a few minutes.'

Now that the moment had arrived, it seemed almost too much to face and Verity followed slowly into the side room off the main ward.

' Here she is at last,' said Mary, and the man sitting in the armchair by the window looked across the room at the daughter he had not seen since that day twenty years ago when he had placed the week-old baby in the arms of his friend's wife. He had not thought then that so many years would elapse before he saw her again, but in the daze of grief and the stunned realisation that he was now responsible for the well-being of his three children, it had seemed the right thing to do at the time.

It was all right; for the moment they looked at each other the years between might never have existed. He saw an almost exact replica of his former wife, and to Verity he was just as she had imagined him. He was quite unlike Guy Blanchard, but there was an immediate affinity between them. She ran to him and knelt beside his chair and there was no need for words.

They were sitting silently hand in hand when Mary returned. ' I'm afraid time's up now, but Dr Soames wants to see me to talk about your coming home.'

John held out his hand to her and for a moment the three were in close harmony and Verity felt that whatever the future held she had now reached a turning point in her life.

It was only afterwards, when she sat downstairs in the crowded waiting-room, that she remembered what her father looked like. He was like an older edition of Robert, she thought. He had the same determined square jaw and firm mouth. His hair was white and, of course, the illness had made him look frail. However, he had that determination which could pull him through, and surely now the worst was over. She grew thoughtful again as she thought of Robert and Sara. She had no doubts about Simon and Dinah. They had accepted her already. Her arrival had been an excitement for them, but she would be very soon taken for granted. The others would be more difficult to win over. It was only natural that they should feel a sort of jealousy, and at that moment Verity resolved that she would try with all her might to make them like her. Her one desire was that they would accept her as their sister and not as a stranger in their midst.

She looked up with a start from her dreaming as Mary spoke to her, and as she rose to her feet she saw that her stepmother was accompanied by a rather portly man in a white coat.

' Our daughter Verity, Dr Soames.'

He took her hand and looked at her closely. It was obvious that he knew the facts. ' I'm glad to meet you, my dear. The one thing we have to concentrate on is that your father should have a long rest and no worry for the next few months. He is in very good shape now and the results of the tests show that there is no need for an operation. A few months' complete rest and freedom from worry about the business will complete the cure.'

After a few minutes, he excused himself and they left by the side entrance. Just as they reached the pavement and were waiting for a lull in the traffic to enable them to go across to the car park, Mary spoke to two people who were approaching.

The man was Garnett Rhodes and he nodded slightly in her direction. He was accompanied by a tall woman who reminded Verity faintly of someone. As her stepmother told Garnett the good news about her husband, Verity suddenly realised that it was Gerard Manley who was like this woman, and the

31

next moment, as Mary introduced her as Margot Manley, she realised that they must be brother and sister.

' Oh, I must introduce you two,' said Mary. ' It's too long a story to tell you now, but this is my step-daughter, Verity. She has been living abroad with friends of her father's.' She smiled warmly at Verity, who felt rather embarrassed. She would have to get used to this sort of thing, and the sooner everyone knew the truth about her now the better.

For a moment as the conversation continued Verity found herself at a loss.

' You know how to keep a secret, Miss Gardner.' Garnett Rhodes looked down at Verity with an expression which she could not interpret. It made her feel as if some apology was called for, and then, remembering his cavalier treatment of her, and the relief which he had shown when Gerard Manley offered to entertain her during the enforced stay in London, she stared back at him with a cool, un-friendly gaze. She didn't make any reply and in a moment or two they had parted company. As they reached the car Verity glanced across the road and saw the two tall figures going up the steps in the hospital. He was listening attentively to his com-panion and just before they entered the open doors he threw back his head and laughed.

' I'm afraid it's going to cause a lot of gossip,' Verity sighed.

' Oh, it won't last long. People soon accept things. It will cause a bit of excitement at first. As long as we can make you happy, your father and I will be satisfied. It's going to be a great change from the sort of life you've been leading.'

' The last five years of my life have been very unexciting. Before that, we travelled a great deal and saw a lot of the world. I had the kindest and most loving guardians. I still think of them as my parents. It's funny,' Verity said thoughtfully, ' I've always wanted to be part of a big family. I used to wish that I had a brother or sister. I think it was a pity that I wasn't told the truth when I was small, but if it made any difference to their happiness, it doesn't matter any more.'

They had reached the house and before they got out of the car, Mary turned to Verity. ' Robert is so worried at the moment. He's young to be in sole charge of the business and, from what Doctor Soames said, it will be a month or two before his father can go back to it. The difficulty is going to be in keeping him away. The only solution seems to be in getting him off for a holiday where he can't get to know what's happening. I'm expecting Robert round as soon as he leaves work to get the latest news, and then we shall have to talk about ways and means.'

' What kind of business it it?'

' It started years ago as a timber yard, but soon after your father left University, where he took a degree in engineering, he had to take over the business on the sudden death of his father and he realised the big future in mass-produced furniture. They produce mostly kitchen equipment and have made quite a name. Robert designs. He never wavered from his desire to go into the business with his father and he studied design. He's a grand boy and his wife is just the kind of girl to help him. Sara will come round. I know she seemed unfriendly, but she's a very good-natured person and, really, she's so wrapped up in her engagement to Michael that she has no time to think about anything else.'

As she finished speaking, and before Verity could reply, there was a kind of war-whoop and round the side of the house ran the two children, Simon and Dinah. They flung themselves at their mother.

'How's Daddy, haven't you brought him home?'

This was Dinah. Simon stood back in his calm fashion. Verity thought she had never seen a young boy with such an air of wisdom. He seemed to have a kind of sturdy independence of thought far beyond his years and she realised that already she felt great affection for him. He wanted his father home just as much as the more volatile Dinah, but he would wait patiently for the time to come without worrying his mother.

'He's a lot better, darlings, and will soon be out of the hospital. He sent his love to you both. Now run along and I'll let Mrs Tennant know we're back. She'll want to get off home.'

The two children had been left in the care of the 'daily' who had offered to stay until they returned from the hospital.

'Here's Robert. He's left work early to hear the latest news. Of course he'll be going in to see his father tonight, but it's important that he should know exactly what to tell him about the business affairs. John must not have any kind of worry at this stage.'

Verity thought Robert looked tired as he left his car and came towards them. Mary rapidly gave him the news and then he said that he must go as his wife was expecting him back early, and later they would go into Leeds to the hospital. Sara found opportunities to go in to see her father during the day as Matron was very understanding and had given permission for her to do this.

'Can I take Verity back with me to tea?'

Mary looked pleased and Verity felt for a minute a warm glow of satisfaction, but then, as she looked at her brother, she had the feeling that his invitation

34

was not so much a desire to become better acquainted as that he had some other motive in making the suggestion.

Dinah was dancing round in her usual ebullient fashion, and Simon stood waiting. It was obvious that Robert was his hero. At last Verity was sitting beside her brother in the car and they were speeding along the country road which led to the outskirts of Leeds where Robert and Laura had a small detached house near to the factory. He was silent for most of the journey and then just as the houses began to crowd more closely together, he stopped the car and turned off the engine.

'I want to have a little talk with you, Verity, and I also want to arrange a time to show you round the factory. Would it be possible for you to come over tomorrow morning?'

'I should like that, Robert.' Verity was indeed interested. She had not talked with her father about his work. It was nice of Robert to make this arrangement, but yet she was puzzled by his manner.

'Is there anything bothering you, Robert?' she ventured at last when the silence had become uneasy.

'It's something I can't confide in anyone but you.' His face looked haggard and old beyond his years. 'Father knows that things are difficult at the factory just now. The recession in trade has hit most people in business. We're having great difficulties at the moment. Verity, you're going to inherit money from your guardian. I would never under ordinary circumstances expect help from you, but unless I can lay my hands on six hundred pounds before September, things may become very serious.'

'I don't understand.'

'I haven't time to explain now. If we don't turn up soon Laura will be anxious, and besides, we have to get to Leeds to see my father.'

'Just a minute, Robert,' Verity spoke slowly. 'I'm not twenty-one until the middle of August and I can't touch anything my guardian may have left me before then.'

'We'll talk again tomorrow.' He started the car and they drove on in silence. Verity's thoughts were whirling. Somehow it seemed too cruel to disclose that, far from being an heiress, she would be lucky to have even a small income when all her affairs were settled. She didn't blame Robert for the misunderstanding and if her guardian had been shrewd in his management of his affairs she would indeed have been able to help without difficulty. As it was, she shuddered to think of Mr Everard's reactions of she asked him to allow her to use any of her small capital.

They had arrived at the small detached house on the outskirts of the town and Laura came running out to greet them. She showed Verity round proudly. They had not been married for much more than a year. Robert had made a good choice. Laura would be a help to him and she was so kind and friendly that Verity felt at home immediately. They left for the hospital at seven o'clock and, after Robert had seen his father, who was still allowed only one visitor at a time, they drove Verity back to Mardale.

'We won't come in,' decreed Robert. 'And be ready at nine-thirty tomorrow. I'll pick you up then and tell Mary I'll take you home to lunch.'

Dinah and Simon were in bed but not asleep and they insisted on seeing Verity before they settled down for the night. She visited Dinah's room first and spent some time satisfying Dinah's insatiable curiosity about her life abroad, and then she went into Simon's room. He was sitting up in bed waiting for her, his red-gold hair damp and sleeked back. She sat on the edge of his bed and they surveyed each other silently for a moment or two.

'I wish Daddy had come home.' The voice was firm enough, but the telltale quiver of his chin showed her that he was close to tears.

'It won't be very long now, Simon,' she assured him. 'I saw the doctor who's looking after him and he says there's no need to worry any more now.'

He gave a sigh of relief, and promised, 'I won't be impatient now, but I got a bit afraid when Mummy and Robert and Sara looked so upset.'

He slid down under the bedclothes and Verity wondered if he would mind if she kissed him, but before she could make up her mind he sat up again and flung his arms around her.

'I do like you, Verity,' and then his eyelids drooped and he was asleep.

Verity joined Mary in the sitting room. The older woman looked a little less tired, but her face still showed the strain of the past weeks when her husband had been so very ill. After a few minutes of conversation they lapsed into a comfortable silence and it was not until nearly ten-thirty that Mary brought up the subject which was uppermost in her mind.

'Dr Soames is insisting on your father having three months' complete rest, and that means we must get him right away. If he is anywhere near the works he won't be able to resist going down to see how things are going. I know that Robert is a bit worried at the moment, but I'm sure he'll be able to sort things out, and so we shall have to arrange that John goes away as soon as he comes out of hospital.'

'Of course he must go away, and you with him,' Verity cried, and then as Mary still looked perturbed, she asked, 'Is it a question of money?'

'That is a big question, but the chief difficulty is

going to be leaving the house and the children. Then there's—'

'I'm another problem,' Verity said thoughtfully, and then, 'Look, you're to tired to worry about it tonight. Somehow we'll find a solution.'

And although Mary was so tired that she slept soundly, Verity scarcely closed her eyes during the long night. Her thoughts whirled round and round, first on the trouble at the works and now this other worry. She fell into a heavy sleep and was late down to breakfast.

Simon and Dinah were just leaving the house when Verity came into the dining room. Mary left her to look after herself as it was time to run the children to school. It was also her day to collect other pupils on her way. The mothers had a rota and Mary coped with two days a week. It seemed a very short time before Mary came back and Robert drove up behind her. Guiltily, Verity ran upstairs for her coat, and noticing that Robert was impatient, she said a swift goodbye and they drove away. This time they did not go right into Leeds but took a side road and finally arrived at the two-story building which was the works.

'Here we are—' Robert said, as he opened the car door and hurried Verity inside. It was an old place, obviously, but many alterations had been done, and everything was spick and span.

'I'll have to go to the office to look at the letters, Verity, but our foreman will take you round until I'm free.'

He took her into the small office, introduced her to the bright-faced girl of about seventeen who sat at the typewriter, and then picking up the telephone he sent for Bill Ellis, the foreman.

Bill Ellis was a square-faced, short and very

broad-shouldered man and Verity felt an instant liking for him. They toured round the factory, which was streamlined from the first room where a boy of about fifteen cut lengths of wood on a simple machine, to the final showroom at the other end of the ground floor.

Bill Ellis proved to be a good showman and his pride in the factory was obvious, as was his concern for news of John Gardner. In his slow broad accent he told her about the various processes, and it was as they came to the end of the tour and Verity had found that Bill Ellis had known her mother that Robert arrived, full of apologies.

'Don't worry,' Verity smiled at her kindly blunt escort. 'Mr Ellis has been a splendid guide and made everything so interesting and clear.'

'Thank you, Bill.'

Robert took his sister's arm and, after a few words about the progress of some work, they left the showroom and returned to the office. The typist brought in coffee and Verity sat by the window as they drank it.

At last Robert spoke. 'Have you given any thought to what I told you last night, Verity?'

She sensed that he was finding it difficult to talk about this trouble and that only the urgency of the problem had driven him to the extreme measure of asking this sister, an unknown quantity to him as yet, for help.

Wildly she searched her mind for some answer which would not sound too cruel or abrupt. She had already told him that she would not have her affairs settled for another month until in fact her twenty-first birthday, but it seemed impossible to disclose the fact that she was far from being comparatively wealthy and, even when the property was sold and the proceeds invested, she would have to earn her own living. It was while her brother waited, his dark eyes lowered and his hand tapping the desk, that she put up her hand to her throat and as she felt the smooth silky texture of the double string of pearls which she wore constantly, a solution of a kind occurred to her.

'Robert—' she rose and came round to stand beside him— 'will you trust me for a week or two? I'm sure I can find the money to help you and to ensure that Father and Mary get that much-needed holiday. It will take me a little time, but I can do it.'

He let out a long breath of relief and then he took her by the shoulders and asked: 'Are you sure, Verity?' and stammered a little. 'I feel such a heel in involving you in our troubles, but it's for my father, Mary and the children. He mustn't get to know about this difficulty. I must fight and use every means of keeping going until he's well enough to take over the reins again.'

They had a long talk and Verity learned how a combination of unfortunate happenings had made this situation arise. A bad consignment of wood had caused them to pull out, and renew a big project at a large building site, and although in time they would receive compensation, it would not come soon enough to meet the six-hundred-pound amount which was due to a firm who threatened to sue for their money.

She could not give any decisive answer until she had consulted Mr Everard. Then her heart sank as she realised the reply he was sure to give. Her future was the important thing to him. No doubt he would sympathise with her brother's difficulties, but she had sensed at their last meeting that he was faintly disapproving of the way her family had left her out of their lives until she was quite grown up. As she struggled to find words to tell Robert this she knew that her first flash of inspiration was the course she must follow.

'I meet Mr Everard in London on August the sixth, the day after my twenty-first birthday.'

'You make me feel an awful heel, Verity.' Robert raised his head and gave her that keen direct look both he and her father shared. 'We ought to be thinking of you and a great celebration, instead of piling our troubles on to you as soon as you arrive.'

'I have an idea, Robert, but it needs some planning. A lot depends on what Mr Everard has to tell me about the estate, but—'

'Your guardian was a wealthy man, though?' said Robert quickly.

'Oh yes, he was wealthy,' she replied dryly, hoping that Robert had not caught the implication of what she had just said.

'It's the possibility that Mr Everard might not approve which is worrying me. He's a dear old gentleman, but not in the least adventurous, and so he might raise some objections. I'm sure, though,' she continued firmly, 'that I can guarantee you the money and also help to send Father and Mary away. In fact, I have a plan about that. If the flat isn't already let it would be a perfect place for them to visit. Have you been to Geneva?'

'No, I've never been abroad at all. I hope in the near future that we shall be able to undertake export orders when this business is settled.'

She rose and smiled up at him.

'I promise I'll have the money for you by the date mentioned. Now I think I'll go into Leeds. Can I get a bus near here?'

'Nonsense, Harry will run you down in the estate

car, and, Verity, you know Yorkshiremen aren't demonstrative, but—'

Words failed him, but with a firm pressure on her arm he took her down to the yard and soon she was speeding into the centre of Leeds. If her plan was to work she must reconnoitre this afternoon and perhaps make a few enquiries.

Harry dropped her at the top of the Headrow and she enjoyed exploring the busy city streets and finding her way about the town. She had told Robert that she would find her way back to the house for lunch and then she was to return to Leeds for another visit to her father. He was getting restive now and soon he would be allowed to leave the hospital. Mary was anxious that arrangements for his long absence from the Works and the holiday should be well in preparation. He would argue, no doubt, but being a reasonable man would see the sense of the doctor's insistence on his complete recovery.

It was now about eleven a.m. and she was gazing thoughtfully into the window of a jeweller's shop when she was startled to hear herself addressed by name.

' What luck, Verity!'

She turned swiftly and felt a sensation of pleasure as she recognised Gerard Manley. She hadn't forgotten those pleasant hours she had spent with him on her first day in England.

' You don't mind me calling you Verity?' He asked the question, but she knew that he was sure of her answer. His blue eyes danced and he looked smart, the complete man about town. In fact, she realised that she had never asked him what he did.

' Come and have some coffee with me. I have half an hour to spare and there's a good little place round the next corner.'

'I'd love to, but I must get the bus back out of Leeds to be at my brother's for lunch at one o'clock. Perhaps you could tell me where the bus station is. I'm not sure how long it will take.'

'Your brother?' For a moment he seemed surprised and then his face cleared. 'Of course, I'd forgotten. I must say it was quite a surprise to me when I found out that you weren't just a visitor.'

They had reached the small café and Gerard seemed to be well known.

'You won't let me miss the bus?' she asked anxiously. 'Laura is driving me in to see my father. Isn't it splendid, he's progressing so well now.'

'I'm very glad for you and of course for the whole family. I don't know whether you've met my sister? She works in the hospital and is a physiotherapist there. I've had news of your father from time to time.'

He kept his word and they walked to the bus station, and, as they chatted, for a moment he seemed about to ask some question. Then he must have thought better of it and although his eyes showed his appreciation of her appearance he made no move to suggest another meeting.

I expect he's a very popular person, Verity thought almost wistfully. Although she had been so happy since her arrival in England she had as yet not had time to explore or to have any kind of social life. After all, she was only twenty and sometimes she felt that she had settled into a rut. It would be fun to go out some evening, to meet young people, to join in activities. She had not for the past few years done anything of a social nature. It had seemed sufficient to care for Guy Blanchard. They had a happy few years, but now she longed for some fun, life, excitement.

She said goodbye to Gerard at the bus station. He apologised for needing to rush off before her bus was due to leave. Verity watched his retreating form and as he turned the corner he looked back with a jaunty wave.

Robert and Laura were waiting for her and after lunch they took another bus back into Leeds.

' It's a nuisance not having the car,' said Laura. ' But it's more important for Robert to take it. Can you drive?'

' Yes,' said Verity. ' But I suppose I should have to take a test before I could drive over here. I had my own car out in Geneva, but I haven't got a British licence.'

' I expect you'll be looking round for a car soon. If I were you I would try for your licence straight away.'

' I'd better wait until I've seen Mr Everard on the sixth of August. I can't do anything without his permission until I'm twenty-one.'

This time both girls were allowed in to see the sick man, though " sick " was hardly the appropriate word now. He looked so much better and Verity could see that his confinement to the hospital was beginning to become irksome.

' I've had a word with Dr Soames and he said there's no reason why I shouldn't come out next week,' he told them.

' Do be careful!' This was Laura, anxious that there should be no setback.

' He'll let me out on condition I go away for a holiday. I don't see how we're going to manage that,' he continued. ' He won't let me go alone and your mother can't leave the youngsters.'

' I can look after them,' said Verity eagerly. ' I'm sure I could manage then.'

44

'No!' her father spoke firmly. 'It's too big a responsibility for you on your own.'

'Sara will be home at night, surely with both of us nothing could go wrong.'

Her father smiled affectionately.

'We'll wait until Mary comes tonight. She usually manages to solve most problems.'

'Perhaps Robert and I could take Simon and Dinah,' Laura broke in.

'I think you have enough on your hands just now,' said John Gardner.

The bell rang for departure and they came out into the broad street. It was about four o'clock.

'Let's have some tea,' suggested Verity.

'If you don't mind, I'll have to get back straight away. Won't you come with me and Robert can drive you back to Mardale later?'

'I think if you don't mind I'd like to have another look round. I didn't see much this morning. I met Gerard Manley and he took me for coffee. I want to explore and find my way about the city and meet Mary when she comes in.'

'Gerard Manley?' Laura sounded surprised. 'I didn't know you'd met him.'

'He took me out in London when I first arrived and Dr Rhodes had to leave me at my hotel to go to the reception.'

Something in the way Verity said this aroused Laura's curiosity.

'Don't you like Dr Rhodes?'

'Oh, I suppose it was a bit of a bind for him to have to look after me, but I can't say that he made a very favourable impression. I can't stand those arrogant bad-tempered types.'

'Oh, I've always thought him exceedingly kind.' Laura was surprised. 'I like him better than Gerard

Manley, anyhow. He—' she stopped.

' He what?' queried Verity.

' Oh, nothing important, he just isn't my type.'

Verity wandered up Briggate, stood at the top of the Headrow and thought what fine shops there were. It was a bright, sunny day and although the buildings did look somewhat grimy the crowds were good-humoured and she felt that she was going to enjoy her stay in this northern county.

After tea Mary came and they went once more to the hospital. John Gardner was in high spirits. For almost the first time Verity saw the great sense of humour and the immense vitality of her father.

' Old Soames says I can come home next week,' he greeted them, his blue eyes gleaming. ' You know it's a lot of nonsense, this business of a holiday. Robert needs me at the Works, he's beginning to look tired. It is a big responsibility for the lad. Of course,' he continued with a note of pride in his voice, ' I know how capable he is, but with a couple of weeks at home and just an occasional potter down to the Works I shall be back in harness in no time at all.'

' Now, John, there's to be no argument about it. You need this break and Dr Soames will see to it that you do as you're told.'

' I have an idea,' Verity broke in shyly. ' I don't think the flat in Geneva is let to anyone yet. I've written to Mr Everard and expect a reply any day now. Don't you see, it's the ideal place for your holiday. Mary can go with you and it will be a break for her too. There's a very good woman who cleaned for us and I'm sure Mr Everard will be able to arrange for her to come in every day. You'll love Geneva and the clear air will be a tonic in itself.

Now don't argue, Daddy.' This was the first time she had used the term which came so easily to the lips of his other children and she saw the look of pleasure on his face.

Mary was looking a trifle rueful, but Verity gave her a warning nod and whatever she had meant to say was lost in the general conversation. It was on the way home that Mary voiced her uncertainties about the scheme.

' You know, Verity, it would be marvellous to go to Geneva, but in the first place I don't think we can afford it, and what on earth should we do with Dinah and Simon?'

' All those things can be sorted out. For instance, you could leave them with me.'

' I wouldn't dream of putting such a charge on you, Verity. They're such scamps, but there is—' and she paused thoughtfully.

' Yes?' said Verity eagerly. ' There is?'

' Well, there's Aunt Emma. I don't suppose the idea of her coming would appeal to the twins, but there's no doubt Aunt Emma would be in her element. She's my only aunt and a bit of a tartar; a good sort really, and she would simply love to be put in charge.'

' Well then, there you are. It's all settled. The flat will cost you nothing, and you'll let me be responsible for the fares out and spending money, of course. You can pay me back when Daddy gets back to work,' Verity added hastily.

' There's an awful lot to discuss,' Mary said, but Verity saw with a feeling of thankfulness that the look of strain had lifted and Mary was smiling happily. They drove home in a contented silence. There was a grey car standing outside the house and, with a jump of her nerves, Verity recognised the vehicle she had travelled down from London in on that miserable first journey to Yorkshire.

'It's Garnett Rhodes!' Mary cried with pleasure, and when they came into the house they found him seated on the floor investigating a fault in Simon's electric train.

As he unfolded his long length and stood up Verity realised that it was the first time she had really looked at him. Oh, of course she had seen him, but not with an inward eye, and she saw now the strong hands, his broad shoulders and massive height; the light grey eyes and crop of dark straight hair. He was good-looking, she had to admit that, but her manner was still cool and reserved as she greeted him.

'Just in time for a cup of tea, Garnett.' Mary was bustling away to the kitchen when he stopped her.

'Sorry, but I must leave now. I stayed to hear the news.'

Mary told him that John was nearly ready to come out of the hospital, and then as he glanced at his watch she said,

'We mustn't keep you, it was good of you to call in.'

'Not at all.' He spoke a little absently and then suddenly he said, looking at Verity, 'I'm driving over the moors to Harrogate tomorrow afternoon. Would you like to come for the ride? You won't have seen much of our lovely countryside yet, I expect?'

Before she could collect her scattered thoughts Mary had eagerly accepted the invitation for her.

'What a splendid idea, Garnett! I've been think-ing that we must try to give her a little more pleasure. All her time so far has been spent in travelling between this house and the hospital.'

. . . . .

Garnett Rhodes had been eyeing Verity with a somewhat sardonic expression and he seemed to be amused as he let in the clutch and they moved off down the drive.

'Look,' he said as they drove out of the gates, 'just come for the ride and enjoy the outing—you look tired out. Are you worried about your father?'

'No.' She could not suppress a sigh and he glanced at her once more.

'Then what's bothering you?'

Suddenly Verity felt a lifting of her spirits. She was conscious of the fact that in contrast to that other journey, she was enjoying herself. With one of her sudden transforming smiles she leaned back and relaxed.

They drove down Pool Bank and up over the moors, branching off towards Harrogate. They came to the new reservoir which had drowned the long-deserted village of West End and he told her the story of the time many years ago when the work in the factories dwindled and people moved away so that in the end the community consisted of only a few farms.

'I used to come through with my father, as a boy,' he told her. 'And it was always a fascinating place for me.'

He stopped the car at the top of a hill and pointed out the various landmarks, telling her of the church and school which were now submerged beneath the waters.

'Wasn't there any protest when this project was mooted?' she asked him.

'You're thinking of the outcry in Wales,' he smiled. 'I don't think it occurred to these hard headed Yorkshire people to make any fuss about something which had to be.'

49

As they drove away Verity looked back at the long stretch of water. The scars of the building still remained, and indeed much work still remained to be completed, but the water had not spoilt the beauty of the valley. Perhaps it was an appropriate end for the once thriving village which had become deserted and ghostlike for many years.

'I'll drop you off at the Valley Gardens, or perhaps you would like to look at the shops?' he said as they drove into Harrogate. 'The Gardens are a showpiece and although coming from Geneva you'll be used to a wonderful display of flowers it might interest you to wander round. I have a call to make on a doctor and it would be boring for you to have to wait outside.'

'I'd love to see the gardens,' Verity replied, and she spent a happy hour, finally seating herself near the entrance and here he found her on his return.

'We won't go into Harrogate for tea,' he said as he drove out again, past the Royal Hall and on to the road to Pateley Bridge. 'There's a little place I know where we can have dinner.'

'Oh, but—' she began, when he stopped her.

'Nonsense. You don't think I'm going to return you to Mary in a state of collapse due to lack of food? Besides,' he continued with a sidelong look, 'you don't really object to another hour or so in my company, do you?'

There he goes again, thought Verity; just as I begin to think he's not too bad after all, he adopts that mocking tone.

'You're very kind,' she said coolly, and missed the twinkle in the glance he gave her.

She had to admit to herself later when they were driving back and nearing home that she had enjoyed the dinner and indeed the whole outing. It was only as they were within a few miles of Mardale that a discordant note arose once more. It was an accidental reference to her meeting with Gerard Manley which seemed to put Garnett Rhodes in a bad humour.

' I shouldn't—' he began.

' Shouldn't what, Dr Rhodes?' she queried icily.

' Oh well, I've nothing against him, but—'

' Don't you think it would be better to say what you really mean rather than this vague sort of accusation? I found Gerard an exceedingly pleasant companion when—' she paused.

He pulled the car into the side of the road and turned to face her, his eyes angry.

' You know that it was quite impossible for me to look after you that evening, and that he turned up by accident. It's unfair to blame me for something I couldn't help.'

' I thought you would be friendly with him,' Verity replied with a sudden change of subject.

' Now what do you mean by that remark?' he considered.

' I thought you knew his sister.'

' That doesn't mean that I—Margot is a different matter entirely.'

' Obviously.' Verity could not keep the note of sarcasm out of her voice. With one part of her mind she wondered wildly why on earth they were at loggerheads. She felt only that the air between them was charged with electricity; that she wanted to hurt this man, childish and petty as it seemed. The way in which he had met her at the airport remained in her memory. She did not care about Gerard Manley; he was friendly, kind, but deep in the heart she knew that he would never appeal in any other way than as a friend.

They were silent for a time and then Garnett

stretched his arm along the seat behind her and spoke.

'I know I have no right to interfere in your private affairs, but I can't let you run into the kind of—' he paused again, seeming to find it difficult to explain. 'You see, Margot Manley is a very fine girl. She's a physiotherapist at the hospital. She has done a lot of good work with my patients, but her brother—'

'Stop!' Verity was in a temper now. 'As far as I'm concerned Gerard Manley is a friend. He has been kind to me when I felt lonely and no one else—' she faltered and to her horror she felt the tears begin to well up in her eyes.

With a sigh he started up the car and they drove on again in silence until they reached the house.

'Will you come in to see Mary?' she asked in a small voice.

He gave her a look which was a mixture of exasperation and something else which she could not define.

'No, it's late. I'll be getting along.'

'Thank you for a very pleasant outing,' She spoke the words like a polite little girl and his lips twitched into an uncontrollable smile.

'Oh, you're the most arrogant, conceited—' Words failed her and she wrenched at the door handle.

Garnett got out at his side of the car and came round to open the door for her. He stood looking down and then taking her by the elbow he escorted her up the steps to the front door.

'I'm sorry little one,' he said in that deep, yet soft voice. 'You're not having a very happy time here, are you? It's a mistake to take a bird out of its gilded cage.'

With a sob of rage she pulled away from him and

found herself standing inside the hall, breathing heavily as if she had run a race. After a minute or two she looked cautiously into the sitting room and saw that Michael and Sara were ensconced on the settee. It was getting dark, and they looked so comfortable and happy together.

'Oh, hello,' said Sara, not moving. 'Mary has gone to bed early with a bit of a headache. Did you have a nice evening?'

Verity murmured a few words, said goodnight and left them. For a long time she sat on the side of the bed. So that was how he saw her, a useless, soft creature who could not compare with his precious Margot. She thought of the years of nursing she had done for Guy Blanchard, the long strain of her foster-mother's illness, and although in a sense it was true that she had never known the need for money, it seemed unfair.

As she drifted off into an uneasy sleep she thought: 'I hate you, Garnett Rhodes, and I'll prove to you that, I'm not just a useless ornamental type!' But even as she thought these words she knew she did not hate him, that he was beginning to occupy more and more of her thoughts.

'I can't,' she whispered to herself, 'I just can't fall in love with him.'

CHAPTER III

'Do me a favour,' said Gerard Manley as he patted his sister Margot on the shoulder. She was hurrying through her breakfast and looked a little annoyed as she answered.

'What kind of favour? Not money, I hope.'

'You've hit the nail right on the head as usual, sister dear.' He spoke in a light, bantering manner.

'You can't possibly need any money. What on earth is it this time? It's only a month since I lent you that last twenty-five pounds and you know what I told you then. No more until you pay it back.'

'We'll have to see if I can't persuade you to change your mind.'

'You haven't been losing it on the horses again? Oh, Gerard!' she sighed. 'You have a good job and salary, when are you going to grow up? It's no use, I can't do a thing about it this time. You'll have to ask Mother.'

'Don't be silly,' he answered sharply. 'Mother would simply discontinue my measly allowance if she thought I so much as went near a racecourse. No, my darling sister, I'm afraid you'll have to come to the rescue again. I'll promise to pay it back this time,' he added coaxingly.

'No, Gerard, quite impossible,' and she returned to her perusal of the daily paper.

'I must hurry,' she remarked a little later. 'I want to see Garnett to arrange about a lift to the meeting tonight.'

'Ah, Garnett,' he replied musingly.

Something in the tone of his voice made her look

54

back at him, she had reached the door.

'What does that mean—" Ah, Garnett "?' she queried.

'You're rather keen on him, aren't you?' he asked. 'Oh, I don't blame you. He's a fine figure of a man and very well-to-do, which is always an added attraction.'

'Garnett and I have a very good understanding of each other. The fact that he has money is as you say an advantage, and once I manage to get this foolish idea of his that he's cut out to be a G.P. out of his head he's going to go far in his profession.'

'I saw him last night.' Gerard was casual.

'Look, Gerard, if you have anything to say, hurry. I'm late now. What does that cryptic remark mean?'

'I happened to be in Harrogate and saw him driving out in the direction of Pateley Bridge, and he wasn't alone.'

'Who?' she demanded.

'The little heiress.'

'Don't talk in riddles! What heiress?'

'Haven't you heard about Verity Gardner, or Blanchard as she's more generally known?'

'You mean that daughter of John Gardner's who's come home from abroad? What do you mean about her being an heiress?'

'Rumour has it that her foster-parents were very high in diplomatic circles and wealthy into the bargain. It might not be a bad idea to carry the friendship I have with her a bit further.'

'Look, I must fly, Gerard,' put in Margot. 'We'll talk about this later.'

'What about the loan?' he wheedled.

'Oh, you're impossible!' she said, but hurriedly

she wrote out a cheque and handed it to him. He glanced at it with a smile of satisfaction and saluted with mock gallantry to her as she left the room.

' I've written to Aunt Emma, as she's not on the telephone, but I'm sure she'll jump at the chance to come,' said Mary to Verity, who was heavy-eyed this morning.

' She loves to organise. I don't think she'll be popular with Simon and Dinah, but a little old-fashioned discipline won't do them any harm. Are you feeling all right, dear?' she asked in a concerned voice.

' I wondered if you would like to come to the prize-giving and sports day at the children's school this afternoon? I must go as Dinah has won a prize for drawing, and Robert and Laura will go in to John tonight.'

' I'd like that.' Verity was reading a letter which had come by the morning's post and she went on, ' I've had a reply from Mr Everard and everything is in order about the flat. He's seeing to it being made ready and says he's looking forward to meeting you both, so now it only remains to arrange for the air tickets as soon as Dr Soames gives the go-ahead signal.'

Mary's face flushed with pleasure and she said,

' I feel so excited about this holiday! It will be the first real break I've had with John for many years, but—'

' Look!' Verity spoke firmly. ' This is to be a real chance for you to have a rest, and I'm sure from what you tell me about Aunt Emma that she will be quite capable of keeping us all in order. You can go away with an easy mind. There is one thing, though. I can't just sit about with nothing to do. I must find myself a job of some kind.'

'There's no need for that, surely, but I see what you mean. It's going to be rather boring for you, especially as you've had no chance to make friends here yet.'

'We'll talk about it later,' said Verity, knowing that Mary had a lot of work to get through before the afternoon. 'Do you mind if I take the bus into Leeds? I want to get the clasp of my necklace mended. What jeweller would you recommend?'

Mary gave her the name of one of the well-known firms in Leeds and Verity set off. She felt more at home in the streets this time and soon found the place she was seeking. She had taken out the jewel case containing her pearls when she first got up that morning and had looked at them for a long time. She remembered the occasion of her eighteenth birthday and the remark Guy Blanchard had made as he fastened the double row of pearls around her neck.

'These were your mother's,' he had said. 'Wear them constantly, pearls deteriorate when they're put away for long. They are my absolute gift to you, and here is the insurance policy. It's paid up for five years. Old Everard knows nothing about these.'

She had wondered if, since Mr Everard had told her how Guy Blanchard had whittled away his capital, that he had known even then that she might be left, not penniless, but unable to live in the style that he had always maintained. She loved the pearls, but weighed in the balance against the needs of her family they had no value for her, and her one thought was to sell them. She felt sure that her foster-father would understand her motives if he were alive, and now the problem was to find the best possible price for them, and to purchase a string which would deceive her family into thinking she still had them. She doubted if anyone had guessed that they were real.

Verity came hesitantly into the jewellers shop. It was not in one of the main streets of the town and was not indeed in any way ostentatious, but there was an air of quiet wealth and good taste in the arrangements of the showcases. An elderly white-haired man came from the back of the shop and as she seemed at a loss for words, he queried:

'Is there anything I can show you, madam?'

'I haven't come to buy,' she answered. 'I really came to see if I could sell something.'

She could tell from his manner that this was the owner of the shop and she thought that he eyed her a little doubtfully, and realised that as usual he was assuming that she was much younger than her proper age.

Without any more ado she opened the case of pearls and put them on the glass-topped counter, and heard the sudden catch of his breath. He picked them up almost reverently and took them to the bright light in the centre of the room.

'I suppose you know that these are extremely valuable?' She sensed he had begun to be suspicious.

She suppressed a slight giggle as she thought that perhaps he took her for some kind of jewel thief.

'Look,' he said, 'come into my office and we can discuss this matter in private.' He beckoned to a younger man who came forward to take his place behind the counter.

The office was a comfortable room and soon she

was seated in front of the big oak desk and the kindly manner of the old gentleman made her tell him her necessity for wishing to dispose of the pearls. She told him everything except of course the reason for needing the money.

He leaned back when she had finished and seemed perturbed.

'You say your solicitor knows nothing of these pearls?'

'No, my foster-father gave them to me absolutely on my eighteenth birthday and he said that there was no need for Mr Everard to be told about it. The insurance is paid up for three years.' She produced the policy and he studied it carefully.

'How old are you now?' he asked, and she told him that in a few weeks she would be twenty-one. He looked relieved.

'Then there's no problem at all,' he said. 'You have only to wait until that date and then you can do as you like about them. I'm not quite sure whether legally you're entitled to sell them now.'

Verity started up in alarm.

'I must have the money now, it's absolutely vital!'

He considered for a long moment.

'I think I can see my way to make you a considerable advance on the pearls, but I must take legal advice on the matter.'

'How long would that take?' she asked anxiously.

'If you can come in at the same time to-morrow I can give you the answer then.'

'Can I leave the pearls with you? I told—' she paused in confusion, then, defiantly: 'I told them I was taking them to have the clasp repaired.'

'Yes, you can leave them in my safe and I'll give

you a receipt for them.'

'Would it be possible for me to have a similar string with the same sort of clasp so that no one need know that I'd sold them?'

'Are you quite sure,' said Mr Collier, 'that you're doing a wise thing? These are very lovely pearls and an artificial string would not give you the same satisfaction in wearing them.'

'I've thought about it carefully,' she assured him, but he caught the hurt look in her eyes.

'Of course you can have a replica made, but we shall have to make a careful copy of the clasp. It may take a week or two.'

'That will be fine,' she said more confidently. 'I shall miss the pearls. I love them, not because of their monetary value but because they were a gift from someone very dear to me, and only the utmost need would make me sell them. It's kind of you to help me in this way.'

She had risen and held out her hand and he took it, holding it for a moment and thinking what a strange thing it was that such a young girl should have to part with a possession she loved. However, it was not his business to query her motives and he had made up his mind to get the very best price possible for them, and to help her in any way he could if his legal advisers proved that this was possible.

'You will keep this an entirely private transaction between us?' she asked anxiously, as he took her through the shop to the main door. She was glad she had his promise because as they reached the door it opened and she came face to face with Gerard Manley.

He looked startled for a minute and then, as Mr

Collier started to introduce them, he said:

'Miss Gardner and I are quite well acquainted. We seem to bump into each other in the most unlikely places.'

'Mr Manley is attached to our firm.' From his tone, Verity sensed that Mr Collier did not altogether approve of his assistant. She wished almost that she had chosen some other jeweller.

'We must make a date for dinner some evening,' Gerard said, and she answered, with the quiet courtesy which singled her out from most girls of her generation, that she would look forward to a meeting. As she said the words she meant them, because he was good company and sometimes she had felt very much alone since her arrival in England.

Gerard was fun to be with; he had a light approach to life, and Verity had begun to wonder if to her family she seemed a very old-fashioned kind of girl. Certainly she had not yet been able to find any point of contact with Sara and she had so longed to have a sister. Robert liked her, she was sure, and she felt at home with Laura but yes, it would be fun to have an evening out with Gerard and she resolved to accept if he telephoned to ask her.

She had a moment's fear that perhaps Mr Collier might let something slip about the pearls, but remembering the kindly old gentleman she knew her secret was safe in his hands. He would not break a promise.

It was fairly late when Verity returned to Mardale and she found the house in a turmoil. Mary was trying to hurry Simon and Dinah through their lunch.

'We shall have to hurry to get back to the school in time,' she said. 'Simon is entered for the obstacle

61

race and some of the swimming sports, and he's on tenterhooks.'

'Don't bother about me,' replied Verity. 'I'll get my own meal, you go and get into your best clothes. The children will expect you to do them credit.'

'We're always neglecting you,' Mary said a trifle guiltily. Once more she made an inward resolution that when things simmered down, when John was fit again and the holiday over, she must see that Verity had a chance to join in some of the youthful entertainments she seemed to have missed in her life abroad. She was so reserved that it was difficult to sum up her character, but Mary had a feeling that under that calm there was a very bright and fiery spirit ready to emerge.

'I'd love to come. Will these things do?'

'Yes!' Mary exclaimed. 'It's a complete mystery to me how you manage to appear absolutely perfectly turned out on every occasion.'

'I've had a good deal of practice in the past,' spoke Verity dryly. 'You don't know how much—' she broke off and didn't finish the sentence and Mary had no time to ask what she had intended to say. In no time the party piled into the car and they sped off to the large house standing in its own grounds which was the school.

'John and I had a little argument about them coming to Miss Pargeter's,' said Mary. 'He thought they should go to the village school like Robert and Sara, but I myself was a pupil here, a very long time ago, and I felt it would be a good thing. I have a great faith in the type of education they're getting, and it's especially suitable for Dinah. Simon will be leaving next year and starting at the local school. They don't take boys here after they're eight years old.'

They had come up the long drive and parked the car at the back of the big buildings. As they walked round to the front entrance to be received with dignity by the formidable lady who was the proprietress and headmistress, the scene was very gay. It was a sunny afternoon, quite hot in fact, and the little children ran about or walked proudly with their parents, showing them the work they had been doing. It was nearly time for the prizegiving to start.

' Ah, Mary my dear!' Miss Pargeter kissed her former pupil's cheek and Verity was introduced to some of the staff, among them the French teacher, Mademoiselle Robert, who was delighted when she discovered that Verity spoke fluent French. In fact she was pretty competent in German and Italian as well.

It was a lovely summer afternoon and after the prizegiving was over Dinah and Simon rushed off to change into shorts. Mary and Verity took their seats near the pavilion on the school playing field. It was a gay sight and everyone was in happy mood as the races started.

Dinah came to sit beside them, flushed with success after winning the girls' hundred yards, and Simon came second in the obstacle race. The crowd cheered as he wriggled under the nets. He was the smallest competitor. It was the swimming, however, which was his chief anxiety. He could hardly wait to pilot his mother and Verity down to the pool.

' I can swim a width of the bath,' he told Verity. ' But of course I'm not in for any of the races. I just want you to see me do it, but we'll have to wait until they've finished.'

After about an hour when most of the contests
63

were over, Simon went to change and came out in his swimming trunks. He looked such a little boy, Verity loved this little brother. She was fond of the others and perhaps if she could break down the barriers she would feel much better, but Simon had accepted her from the first.

' Watch now, Verity! ' called Simon, and she duly concentrated her attention on his slow progress across the pool and was round at the other side to give him a helping hand out.

' If you'll wait until Simon is dressed, Verity, I think I'd better get back up to the lawn and find a table for tea. They're sure to be having it out of doors on such a hot day. I'll get hold of Dinah and we'll wait for you. Don't be too long.'

Verity sat beside the now deserted pool. It was quite a distance away from the main building, but the drive leading up from the main gates was not very far away. She had just begun to wonder if she had better go in search of her brother when she saw a car coming through the gates. She realised that the driver was Dr Rhodes and beside him, looking very cool and attractive, Margot Manley. The doctor glanced towards the pool and at that precise moment Verity saw the tiny figure of a little girl running full tilt down the slope which led to the other side of the bath. Simon had come out of the dressing rooms and stood unable to move. Without giving herself time to think Verity threw off her shoes. There was not time to run round to the other side of the pool and at the rate the child was running nothing could prevent her from falling into the water at the deep end.

Verity flew up the low springboard and her slender figure flashed out in a splendid dive, and she came up nearly across the width of the baths just as the child toppled into the water. It was only a few yards' swim and then Verity had her in her arms and held her above the water. Simon had run round by now and was vainly trying to lean down to reach her, but Verity gasped out instructions for him to get away from the side.

Then she felt a strong hand grip hers and the little girl was taken from her grasp. There were quite a number of people about now. The child's mother had appeared and was sobbing incoherently. Then everyone was silent while Dr Rhodes placed the child on the grass and turned her over on to her face.

' She's all right,' he said eventually. ' She hadn't really gone under when Verity got to her. Someone get a blanket and I'll take her to the hospital for a check-up.' Turning to the mother he said: ' I'm absolutely certain she's not hurt in any way, but what on earth was she doing running about alone like that?

The mother burst into tears.

' She was with her older sister and somehow Jane got distracted for a minute and Maria ran away. She was down here with me earlier watching the races, and she loves to paddle and bathe.'

Verity had realised that she must cut a funny sight, her wet dress clinging to her, so she disappeared into one of the dressing rooms. She discarded her wet things and finding a towel drying on a heated rail she had a good rub down and hung her things to dry on the rail.

I'll just have to wait here until they dry, she thought, and she was not displeased at the idea of remaining out of sight until the fuss died down. As she passed Simon she whispered hurriedly to him that

65

he must go for his tea and tell his mother that Verity would not be coming back up to the school to join them and that she would see them later. She had made up her mind to find her way home on foot as soon as it was possible to get dressed again.

She felt very much better when she was dry again and her dress was very little the worse for wear; the nylon things were drying rapidly and she sat contentedly waiting, thankful only that her action in diving in had been successful, that the child was safe.

Presently she found that she could wear her clothes and when she was ready and had made herself as tidy as possible she emerged into the sunlight. Everyone had disappeared, she found thankfully, and she made her way out on to the road. It hadn't seemed far to the school in the car, but she hadn't really taken any note of the route, so she walked along the path in what she hoped was the direction of Mardale. There were a few houses further down the road surely someone would direct her.

Meanwhile, up at the school Simon had found his mother, but she was rather put out because he was by himself and did not listen to his rather garbled account of what had happened. Tea was over now and hurriedly she made Simon eat up the plateful she had kept for him, and was a little annoyed because Verity still did not appear. Miss Pargeter had been over to talk to her earlier and she was intent on seeing Verity and telling her of a scheme which seemed to be the right one to solve the problem of finding a post for Verity while they were away in Geneva. It was only when the father of the little girl who had been so nearly drowned came to ask for Verity that she found out what had really happened.

' I don't know where my stepdaughter can be,' she

said anxiously. 'Simon, why didn't you tell me?' His bottom lip quivered and she remembered with a pang of remorse that she had not given him much chance to say anything at all.

'My wife and I would like to say thank you in person,' said Mr Gooding. 'My wife has just telephoned from the hospital and Maria isn't a bit the worse, but if your daughter hadn't been so prompt and quick-thinking there would have been a tragedy.'

'I wonder where Verity can be now?'

'She told me to say she would go home as soon as her things were dry.' This was Simon, who managed to get his message delivered at last.

'How on earth was she going to find her way back?' Mary was agitated now. 'I'm sorry, Mr Gooding, but I must get home and perhaps you can meet my daughter later and thank her for yourself, though I'm sure she wouldn't want any great fuss.'

Hurriedly making her farewells to Miss Pargeter, and promising to get in touch with her as soon as possible, she piled the children into the car.

Verity had nearly reached the first row of cottages when a sports car drew up beside her and the light voice of Gerard Manley spoke.

'Can I give you a lift?'

'Oh, Gerard!' she cried thankfully.

'Jump in.' He opened the door.

'Would you mind running me home? I want to get changed as quickly as possible.'

'You look very nice as you are. Going somewhere?'

'No, but I'm just a little damp. I can't explain, but I was watching the swimming sports at Miss Pargeter's and—'

67

' Some silly little chump splashed you. Of course I'll run you back.'

' I'm not taking you out of your way, am I?'

' No, I'd finished for the day and was on my way home. I say, Verity, this is a good opportunity. Are you doing anything tonight? We might as well take this chance of going out to dinner.'

' I don't know if Mary has any plans—'she hesitated.

' Oh, come on, I feel like a celebration.'

' Has something good happened to you at work?' she asked.

He laughed. ' Something good? Yes,' and he patted his breast pocket, but did not explain that for once he had backed a winner at the races.

It was at this moment as they were laughing heartily that Dr Rhodes' car passed them and he spoke to Margot, sitting beside him.

' Wasn't that your brother with Miss Gardner?'

' I didn't notice, but I suppose it could have been Gerard. He had arranged to come to Miss Pargeter's on his way home from Leeds. You know my sister Jane's little boy is a pupil there and Gerard was supposed to be coming to watch the sports.'

' It looks as though he changed his mind. It was definitely your brother in that car.'

' Oh well, you know Gerard, and he's quite taken with little Miss Gardner—been seeing quite a bit of her, I believe.'

Garnett Rhodes gave an exclamation of annoyance.

' I should have made sure someone took care of her, but it was important to get the child to hospital. That was quite a feat she performed in diving across the baths, and quick thinking too.'

Margot glanced at his profile, which looked decidedly grim.

' I shouldn't worry, and it wasn't such a wonderful thing really. She's obviously a good swimmer, almost bound to have had a lot of practice. I heard she lived in Geneva before coming to Mardale.'

' Practice or not, that doesn't alter the fact that she thought quickly and saved that little girl from what could have been a fatal accident.'

Margot looked as if she were about to make some tart reply, but evidently she thought better of it and they continued on their way back to Miss Pargeter's in silence.

Everything seemed to be over now and people were making their way home with their children. Mary was standing on the main doorstep talking earnestly to her old headmistress.

' I'm awfully sorry,' she said. ' I can't think what's happened to Verity, but I'll send her up to see you tomorrow. I'd better get home now.'

Dinah and Simon had been waiting patiently and as Garnett Rhodes and Margot drove up Mary greeted them hastily and then prepared to make her way to the car.

Garnett Rhodes hastened to tell her that Verity was on her way back to Mardale, and he also gave her a full account of the happenings of the afternoon.

' I shouldn't worry, Mrs Gardner.' Margot was cool in her manner. ' My brother was driving her home and from the glimpse we caught of them they were enjoying themselves.'

' I thought you hadn't noticed them?' This was said in a dry tone by Garnett, and Margot coloured slightly and then tried to change the subject by talking to Miss Pargeter and apologising for her late arrival. She too had been a pupil at the school.

'Come along, we must get home now. If Verity was in the water as you say, what on earth did she do? She must be soaking wet. I know it's a warm day, but I shan't rest until I see she's all right.' Without any further ado she started the car and drove off.

'Are you coming, Margot?' Garnett sounded preoccupied. 'I think we'd better visit the Gardner household and make sure Verity is no worse for the ordeal.'

'Oh, for goodness' sake!' She sounded pettish. 'You said she was talking to Gerard, so she must be perfectly all right. She obviously is a very good swimmer, and after all, she only handed the child out of the water.'

'That's a bit unfair.' He sounded distant again and Margot knew that she had gone too far.

'Oh well, if you won't be satisfied,' she murmured, and they were silent until they reached the Gardner household.

Verity had changed and was looking as cool and fresh as usual, and it did seem as if Dr Rhodes was unduly concerned, but he made his apologies for forgetting her plight.

'It didn't matter,' the girl replied. 'I know everyone was concerned for the child. Are you sure she's quite unhurt?'

'They gave her a clean bill at the hospital and she was lively enough when I left them. By the way, I expect you will be receiving a visit from her parents. They want to thank you.'

Verity coloured. 'Oh, I do hope not, it was nothing—just lucky that I was waiting for Simon to change. I'm so used to the water it was no hardship to me.'

'Very quick thinking all the same,' and the grey eyes smiled into hers.

'If we're going out for dinner, Verity, we'd better be pushing off.' This was Gerard, who had been waiting impatiently.

'Don't you think,' broke in Mary, 'that it would be better to stay at home tonight? You must have had a bit of a shock, after all.'

'Oh no. I've had a bath and changed my clothes. I was a trifle damp and it was a good thing Gerard came along in time to run me home.' She smiled at Gerard in her most dazzling way, unable to resist the temptation to show Dr Rhodes that his concern for her was unnecessary. At the back of her mind she realised that the sight of him with Margot, who seemed to be his constant companion, was upsetting her.

She climbed gracefully into the sports car beside Gerard who was looking impatient.

'What on earth was all that fuss about?' he queried. 'Rhodes with a face like thunder, and Margot didn't seem too happy either.'

Verity laughed. 'It's funny now, looking back, but at the time it could have been a tragedy.'

'Stop talking in riddles and tell me what really happened. I gather that you performed some kind of rescue. So that was why your clothes were damp?'

Sketchily she gave him her version of the affair.

'It was nothing; your sister was right—such a fuss! I'm a very good swimmer and I'm thankful the child came to no harm. She was a dear little thing.'

Gerard too began to laugh and then he was serious.

71

With a sideways look at the girl's enchanting profile he said:

'He's a bit of a dull stick, Garnett. I often wonder how I shall get along with him when—'

'When what?' as he did not continue.

'Oh, it's a pretty foregone conclusion that he and Margot will make a match of it. They meet a great deal at the hospital and I've never known him take any notice of any other woman.' Except you, he thought to himself, and if I'm to keep in with Margot any nonsense of that kind will have to be nipped in the bud. Besides, it's not a bad idea if the little girl from Geneva does turn out to be an heiress. I must find out more about her.

He was a gay and charming companion and they dined and danced at a well-known hotel in Leeds. He talked amusingly and managed in his clever fashion to draw from Verity a good deal of information, but he had the sense to realise that she would resent any discussion of her private affairs. Never mind, there were ways of finding out, and he thought back to the day he had seen her in the jeweller's shop. No good asking his elderly partner, but it should be possible to find out why Verity had left her pearls.

As they drove home later that night Verity was silent. She had laughed, danced and enjoyed herself, but a mood of sadness seemed to fall upon her. She tried to shake it off and respond to Gerard's gay nonsense.

'We'll do this again often,' he remarked as they stopped outside the house in Mardale. There was a light on in the sitting room and Verity was stricken with remorse as she wondered if Mary had waited up for her, and then there had been something said about Miss Pargeter. She wished now that she had not rushed off so hurriedly. Then she remembered that Gerard had done his best to entertain her and she answered gaily:

'Of course I'd love to, but I really must hurry in now.'

He let her go. No time yet to make any advances. He sensed that she had withdrawn from him. Time enough, he would draw her into his set and earn Margot's gratitude by keeping Verity out of her way.

He went up the steps with her and lightly kissed her forehead.

'Goodbye, Princess.'

'Why do you call me that?' she said, startled.

'Oh, you're like someone out of a fairy tale, so fair, so fragile. And—' she did not catch the words he murmured under his breath—'so unawakened.'

Mary was waiting by the stairs when Verity let herself in.

'You needn't have waited up for me,' said Verity as she saw how tired the other woman looked.

'I didn't really. I was trying to catch up with some of the mending and odd sewing jobs which have piled up while John has been ill, and I fell asleep. When I woke up a moment ago I was thankful to hear you come in. Have you enjoyed yourself?' She looked at the girl's face and thought that she did not look particularly happy.

'I wanted to tell you about something Miss Pargeter said to me this afternoon, but it can wait until tomorrow. Come along to bed now.' And she put on the upstairs light and they went slowly up the stairs together.

As they parted at the top of the stairs Verity asked:

'Was I rude to Dr Rhodes and Miss Manley? I

felt afterwards as if I'd been a bit abrupt, but I didn't want any fuss. No one's life was in any danger.'

' I'm afraid you'll have to have the ordeal of meeting Maria's father and mother. They rang up and are coming round tomorrow evening to thank you personally. They asked me to tell you that she's as lively and up to mischief as ever.'

' I'm so glad, but I wish I needn't have to talk about it. It was so silly, really, and I must have looked such a fool to—' She stopped and Mary looked at her curiously. It was only when Verity got into her own room that she finished the sentence in her mind.

' I must have looked a bit of a show-off doing that racing dive, but it seemed the best thing at the time.'

She slept finally, but the memory of Margot Manley's mocking look remained with her and as her eyes closed she remembered the smiling grey ones and the gentle way the doctor had spoken to her, and wished that she had been a little more friendly.

CHAPTER IV

There were letters for both Mary and Verity the following morning.

'This is from Aunt Emma. As I thought, she's delighted to come and take charge.'

There was a concerted groan from the two children and Mary tried to look severe.

'Oh, it won't be so bad,' she declared. 'And you do want Daddy to have this holiday and come back quite well again.'

'She's so bossy,' said Dinah.

'Is she bossy? What does it mean?' Simon looked puzzled.

'She's very kind really, and you must try to be good and not cause any bother while she's here,' said their mother.

Verity had been listening absently to the conversation as she read her letters, one of which was from Mr Everard. For the first time she had something concrete to go on about her affairs.

He had obtained probate of her guardian's will and she was the sole beneficiary. From his preliminary account, she found that in all there would be about two thousand five hundred pounds in cash and the flat, which Mr Everard proposed she should let in order to bring in some income. Her spirits rose. It sounded a lot of money, but then, as she read further and found that when it was invested it would bring in only a small amount of interest, she felt again that the selling of the pearls was the only way. Yet she felt curiously guilty. Mr Everard had been so good and kind; he had her very best interests at

75

heart and it seemed almost impossible to do this thing without first talking it over with him. She decided that she would go into Leeds today and see the jeweller and find out what he really thought about the matter.

To Mary she said:

' I'm to meet Mr Everard in London on the sixth of August and he suggests that he makes the plane reservations for you and Daddy, and that you travel to Geneva with him. He'll be staying in London about a week.'

' That's a very kind idea.' Mary looked relieved. She had done so little travelling that she had rather dreaded the responsibility of getting John safely over the journey.

' I must meet him in London, so I'd better make plans,' Verity went on. ' It's only a fortnight from now.'

' You'd better stay at the same hotel as before—that is, if you can get in. It will be busy in August.'

' No!' Verity was sharp, and Mary looked up in surprise. ' It's too expensive. I'd rather go to some cheaper place.'

Mary was a little bewildered, but she changed the subject.

' I never got the chance to talk to you yesterday, in all the excitement, about Miss Pargeter.'

' Miss Pargeter?' With an effort Verity tried to collect her thoughts.

' Yes—you know, dear, you said you wanted to do some kind of work while we were away, and something the French mistress said gave me an idea.'

' Mademoiselle Giravd?'

' Yes, it was while we were at tea that Mademoiselle Giravd joined us, and it seems that she's very worried because her elderly mother needs her at home for a while. The younger sister who is usually in charge is ill. It occurred to Mademoiselle Giravd that you might be able to fill her place for the six months or so that she'll be away in Paris.'

' But I never—'

' I know what you're going to say, you've never taught before, but then these are very small children and you have such a very good accent. A pity you have no qualifications as, of course, it will mean much less pay, but after all, it's more the chance to occupy yourself which is your concern, isn't it?'

' Oh well, yes, in a way.' Verity sounded so doubtful that once again Mary was puzzled.

' There's no need to decide in a hurry. After all, school is finished for seven weeks and you'll have to wait until the beginning of next term. You could go and see Miss Pargeter and have a talk, she was quite enthusiastic about the idea. It will be difficult for her to find a replacement for Mademoiselle Giravd.'

' It does sound a possibility. And then, of course, I did study French at the University in Geneva. I took the advanced course, but that doesn't qualify me to teach.'

' There you are!' Mary was delighted.

' I'll certainly see Miss Pargeter, but not just yet. I want to go into Leeds this morning—I have to see about my necklace. Is there any shopping I can do for you?'

' No, you run along, and I must get the room ready for Aunt Emma. She'll be arriving in a couple of days, and I'd better prepare Mrs Tennant a bit. I do hope they get on, Mrs T. is such a treasure.'

' I'll try to keep the peace between them,' said Verity. ' I only hope Aunt Emma will approve of me.'

'She'll be a bit surprised. I don't think she ever knew of your existence. I haven't seen very much of her since my marriage and the subject never came up.'

Verity felt as if she now had another awkward situation to face. She wondered if her father would remember that she would be twenty-one on the fifth of August. She could not remind him. Of course she had told Robert, but he had been in such a state of preoccupation with his worries that she doubted if he had taken in what she had said. It would have been nice to have had a proper birthday celebration. She sighed as she went to catch the bus.

Mr Collier was in when she arrived at the shop and took her once more into the comfortable back room. She caught a glimpse of Gerard who was showing a fine collection of Georgian silver to a prosperous-looking couple, obviously American.

When she was seated, Mr Collier looked at her with a rather worried expression.

'My dear Miss Gardner,' he said, 'I find myself in a rather difficult position. I really think you should wait until after your twenty-first birthday before selling the pearls and I do strongly advise you to think a very good deal before taking such a drastic step. You say you are in urgent need of this money, but it will take me quite a time to find the right customer.'

Verity was conscious of a sense of relief. This settled the matter. She had enough in the bank for the air fares to Geneva, and the rest of the money she could supply later. There was no other course but to tell Mr Everard that she did not want the money invested for her. She would hate to shock the dear old man, but after the fifth she could do as she liked. She did not want to tell him the reason for needing to keep it herself. She could not be disloyal to her family.

Meanwhile, having finished with his customers, Gerard was consumed with curiosity and, without attracting the attention of the assistant, he had managed to pass the slightly open door of the back room and heard several titillating bits of the conversation. So Verity was trying to sell her pearls! He remembered now that she had told him that she had left them to be repaired.

He caught only snatches of the talk. At one point she was saying quite vehemently: 'No one must know about this, Mr Collier.' The little heiress was perhaps not so wealthy after all, he mused. Better not to tell Margot. He could string her along nicely by promising to keep Verity out of Garnett Rhodes' company, and the fact that he knew something about Verity's affairs which she wished to keep secret would give him some sort of advantage in his dealings with her. He knew she was not attracted to him in any romantic way. Gerard was nothing if not a realist.

The next fortnight seemed to fly. It had been decided that only on the day before their departure should John Gardner come home from the hospital as it would have been impossible to keep him from making a trip down to the factory to see for himself what was afoot. Aunt Emma arrived. Curiously, she was not a bit like the dragon Verity had visualised, but rather formidable all the same.

She was not at all elderly in her appearance, although Mary had said she was in her late sixties.

She had dark hair streaked only slightly with grey and a pair of piercing dark eyes, an aquiline nose and a very trim, erect figure. She was also extremely smartly dressed. She had taken the news about Verity, the newcomer to the family, without batting an eyelid.

Dinah and Simon were still a bit in awe of her. It was holiday time and they were used to running in and out and tearing about the garden. So far Aunt Emma had made no comments on their behaviour, but they rather dreaded the thought of the time their mother would be gone. One thing was certain, John and Mary could go away with an easy mind. Aunt Emma would be in full control.

The morning of the fifth of August had come. Robert had offered to take Verity to the station, but the train did not leave until twelve-fifteen. Her suitcase was packed and ready and she was wearing the string of artificial pearls which Mr Collier had provided for her. He had kept the real string to re-thread and she had thought herself that it would be a good idea to wear the false ones for most occasions. She would wear the original string at night to keep them in condition, but she felt that perhaps she had been taking rather a big risk in using them so constantly. No one had noticed the substitution and if her first plan had been put into action, no questions would have been asked. She felt much better now, though, that she was going to be open with Mr Everard.

She ran downstairs and became aware of a subdued giggling, and then she opened the dining-room door and the chorus began:

' Happy birthday to you, happy birthday to you,

happy birthday, dear Verity, happy birthday to you!'

Dinah and Simon rushed to hug her and Mary kissed her. There was a pile of cards and parcels beside her place at the table, and even Aunt Emma beamed in an unaccustomed manner.

As she opened the cards, one by one, she found that everyone had remembered her, and best of all was the little parcel and letter from her father and Mary. How could she have wondered if he would forget? Her eyes filled with tears she could not control as she looked at the beautiful pair of antique earrings in the tiny box. There was also the even more precious long letter from her father in which he explained how he had never forgotten for one moment each year her birthday, but the fact that his friends had not chosen to tell her of his existence had prevented him from sending her a reminder. Mary was smiling and the two children watched excitedly as Verity came at last to their little gift.

' Just exactly what I wanted!' she cried, hugging them both as she looked at the rather gaudy sponge bag.

' We chose it ourselves,' said Dinah importantly.

' Do you really like it, Verity?' Simon was leaning against her chair and looking earnestly into her face.

' Of course, darlings, and all the other things besides. I've never had such a wonderful surprise. I didn't know any of you knew about it.'

' Twenty-one is very old, isn't it?' This was Simon, looking as though he expected Verity suddenly to develop grey hair. They all laughed at this and then Mary remarked:

' When we get back from Geneva we'll have a real celebration, at Christmas. I've been longing

for an excuse for a party. But I've made a cake,'
she continued. 'It's a pity you won't be here at tea-
time, but we'll cut it just before you go off for the
train.'

Verity had in the end changed her mind and booked
in the hotel which held such very uncomfortable
memories for her. It had been easier than to look
for another unknown place, and Gerard had been
helpful here because his mother was such a regular
patron that they had managed to squeeze Verity in
for the few days she needed. It would enable her to
complete her business with Mr Everard and to see
her parents off at the airport.

On the morning of the sixth of August she
wandered about London restlessly. She tried to
enjoy visiting some of the art galleries and shops, but
she was turning over and over in her mind the way
in which she was going to ask the solicitor to hand her
capital over to her. It seemed an eternity until the
moment when she came down into the lounge for tea
and found him waiting. He, too, had a little parcel
and she was touched as she looked at the tiny musical
box key ring, one of the things the Swiss make so
well. She wound it up and pulled out the little knob,
and the sound of the tinkling notes brought back a
wave of longing for another sight of the town, the
lake, and the splendid view of Mont Blanc which she
had seen so many times from the balcony of the flat.

As they sat down, and he took out a large bundle of
papers from his notebook, Verity felt her heart begin
to pound. What if she was unable to convince him
that she was determined to have the money? After
he had adjusted his reading spectacles and raised
his eyes to look at her, Mr Everard said in some

alarm:

'What on earth is wrong, my dear? You've gone very pale. I know,' he said soothingly, 'that it must be a bit of a shock to you to find that you have so small an income, but surely now that you have the backing of your family it's not as serious a matter as it might have been?'

'I'm perfectly all right,' she stammered. 'Please go on, and let me know the full details.'

She couldn't listen, though; her mind was set on the awful moment when she would have to ask him outright for the money. Better, perhaps, if she went back to Mardale without saying anything and obeyed her first impulse and sold the pearls, and then, with a set to her mouth which gave her an uncanny resemblance to her father, she interrupted the old gentleman.

'I don't want you to invest this money for me, Mr Everard. If it's possible, I want it transferred to my bank account here in England. And by the way,' she hurried on, 'I've got the chance of a post at a school near my home, so there's no need to worry about my future.'

His jaw dropped in intense surprise as he tried to digest this sudden statement.

'Please, please, Mr Everard, do trust me. I'm entitled to do what I like with this money?'

'Yes, of course,' he answered slowly. 'But I had hoped that you would be guided by me in this matter.'

'It will be all right,' she assured him. 'In a few months I'll let you have it back to invest for me. I'm sure I can safely promise that.'

The elderly man took off his spectacles and polished them thoughtfully.

83

'Are you sure, Verity,' he said at last, 'that you're not in some kind of trouble? You know you can rely on me and I would not betray your confidence.'

'I can't explain now, Mr Everard. You'll just have to trust me. It's nothing like that at all.'

He sighed. 'Then in that case there is nothing more to be said. I'll make the arrangements, and before I go back to Geneva you shall have the cheque for the full amount.'

She sat back and closed her eyes. The worst was over now, but, stealing a look at her old friend, she could not help wishing that it was possible to be open with him. For her own part it would not have mattered, but she felt instinctively that it would be a great blow to her father's pride if the truth came and, also, Robert had to be protected. He did so want to make a success of his management of the business. She could now pay off the six hundred pounds for him and also provide the money which he could pass on to his parents for the holiday and the expenses of running the home while they were away.

At their next meeting on the following day, after various formalities were over, she found herself tucking the precious cheque safely away in her handbag and there was a slightly forced atmosphere as Mr Everard said goodbye. She would see him again at the airport on the following day.

Yet when she arrived and found her father and step-mother already in the lounge with their old friend, the chief feeling she had was one of surprise and another emotion she could not quite define. Garnett Rhodes was one of the party and it was soon explained that he had offered to drive them up to London. Dr Elliot had thought it would be a more comfortable journey for John Gardner.

Verity found that her father looked so much better, almost she thought as he must have done before his sudden illness, and Mary sparkled with delight mixed with anxiety that all should go well in her absence. She spent the time before the plane departed giving Verity last-minute instructions and then she relaxed and said:

' I'm not going to worry any more. This is the most exciting thing that's happened to me for a very long time. Do you realise this is the first time I've been abroad; the first time I've flown? It's the first time for many things.'

Their flight was called and the last goodbyes made. Mr Everard was stern, but his voice was kind as he assured Verity that he would always be at her service if she needed to get in touch with him. And then they were gone, out to the gleaming jet which waited on the runway, and Verity found herself once more alone in familiar surroundings with Garnett Rhodes. They stood together on the outside balcony and saw her parents board the aircraft. Then it was off, taxiing until out of sight, and finally they saw it airborne, and turned away.

It was nearly quarter to eight. The flight had been scheduled for seven-thirty and had left practically on time. Garnett Rhodes glanced at his companion. They had not spoken to each other much in the bustle of departure.

' I suppose,' he said, ' that you'll be staying another night in London?' His tone was formal.

' Yes, I have a room at the Garton,' she replied in more or less the same stilted manner.

They had come out of the airport now and Verity turned to him, saying:

'Thank you, Dr Rhodes, for your kindness in bringing my parents up to London. It made things so much easier for them. I'll make my own way back to London.'

'Nonsense!' he admonished, and taking her arm he led her firmly towards the car park. Once again she found herself riding with him in the grey Jaguar.

'I'll take you back into London, of course,' he said, and for a while he concentrated on getting clear of the traffic. It was a lovely summer evening and everyone seemed to be out and about.

'I'm staying in town tonight too,' he remarked at last, and then he threw back his head and began to laugh.

Verity was indignant. 'You might tell me what's so funny!'

'I was just thinking,' he said more seriously, 'that it's absurd the way we seem to be at loggerheads each time we meet. I can't imagine why.'

Verity smiled. 'I think we got off on the wrong foot. After all, you can't say you made my welcome to this country a very happy occasion, and I seem to have to keep apologising for being a nuisance.' She continued firmly:

'This time, you have no need to upset any of your plans. I'm quite capable of taking care of myself now.'

She could not help poking fun at him because on that first meeting he had thought her so much younger than she really was.

'After all, I'm twenty-one now and therefore I shall be safe enough in the big city on my own—and especially at the Garton.' She chuckled as she thought of that haven of respectability.

'When were you twenty-one?' he asked so curtly

86

that she stole a glance at him in case one of his frequent changes of mood had overtaken him.

'Yesterday,' she replied, and then wished she had not brought the subject up.

'That settles it,' he said. 'This does call for a celebration. I'll drop you at the Garton and pick you up in an hour. We'll go out. It's a bit late for the theatre, but we can dine and, in fact, we'll do whatever you would like. I'm not taking any refusal.' Then, coaxingly, he added: 'Come on, let your hair down for once and forget I'm the enemy.'

They had arrived at her hotel now and, as Verity still hesitated on the pavement, uncertain whether to maintain her promise to herself to keep from being involved with this man, he provoked her to speechless anger once more.

'You can pretend you're with Gerard,' he said, 'but don't be a minute longer than an hour. I'll be back.' And he drove away leaving her looking after the car with a mixture of exasperation and also another nameless kind of flutter of her senses.

When Verity reached the privacy of her hotel bedroom, she took out again the cheque for two thousand five hundred pounds which Mr Everard had so reluctantly handed to her. She had known that he was bitterly disappointed in her decision to use the money and no doubt as the plane sped back to Geneva he would be contemplating the folly of the younger generation. She hoped that soon she would be able to go to him and hand back the full amount for him to invest as he wished. She was thrilled, though, by the thought that she would have good news for Robert on her return to Mardale next day.

Now to decide what to wear. She felt a rising sense of excitement. That evening with Gerard had been pleasant, but every minute spent in the company of the enigmatic Garnett was a challenge. She wore a dress of blue wild silk and the cultured pearls. She piled her hair high and used plenty of eye make-up, and hoped that for once she looked sophisticated. Garnett Rhodes watched her coming downstairs towards him and smiled indulgently, but with admiration. In spite of her reminder that she was now twenty-one she still looked so terribly young and in some subtle way very vulnerable.

It was a glorious evening. They dined and danced and afterwards they walked through the streets back to the hotel.

It had been so fresh and cool after the warmth inside the large hotel that it was by mutual consent that they had left the car and walked. Verity had a light silk coat to match her dress and his hands seemed to linger as he helped her into it. As they walked she told him of her plan to teach at Miss Pargeter's the next term, and he had approved, although still slightly sceptical, she felt, of her ability.

' I do agree,' he said, ' that it will be much better for you to have some kind of work. It will take a little getting used to, I expect, after—'

' After what?' Her voice was sharp. This was the first discordant note in the whole evening and she felt bitterly disappointed. Without talking too much about herself and her life in the past she could not tell him that she was not the spoilt heiress that everyone imagined.

' Sorry!' His face creased into that smile which so illuminated his face. ' I'll be good.'

But the damage was done. She felt as if he were

mocking her. They walked the rest of the way in silence and once again she vowed inwardly that this was the very last time she would allow herself to be upset by an encounter with him. She stole a sideways look at him and found to her annoyance that he was looking down at her with that quizzical look which had become familiar. I wonder, she thought irrelevantly, if all his women patients fall in love with him, and felt herself blushing.

During dinner he had asked the waiter to let him know if there was a telephone call for him, and just before they finished the meal he had been called away. When he returned he had seemed preoccupied, but had not enlightend her as to the nature of the call.

Now as they stood at the reception desk and waited for the night porter to hand over her key he started to speak, but stopped as the porter turned round and handed it over the counter.

'I'll see you up to your door,' he said, taking the key and leading her across to the lift.

'It's not necessary—' she began, but they were now gliding silently up to the third floor, and they walked in silence along the thickly carpeted corridor to her room. It was very late and only a dim light burned at the end of the landing.

He looked down at her.

'I'd like to offer you a lift home tomorrow in the car,' he said, 'but that phone call I had was from someone I have to help to choose some hospital equipment and I shall not be able to leave early.'

'Don't worry about me,' she answered coolly enough. 'I have my ticket for the Pullman and I'm anxious to get home as soon as I can. I don't want to leave Aunt Emma alone to cope with the children any longer than need be.'

As she got ready for bed she thought about the evening. She had enjoyed it; every minute spent in the presence of Garnett Rhodes was important to her. As she climbed into bed, tired but happy, she thought with regret that it would have been wonderful if he had been able to take her back to Mardale.

Her train left at eleven the following morning and she ordered a taxi to take her to Kings Cross. She had very little luggage and it was another glorious day.

Her spirits rose. There would be many opportunities of seeing the doctor in Mardale. She had at last admitted to herself the fact that this man meant a great deal to her, that in fact she was falling hopelessly in love with him. It was while the taxi was held up at a crossing that she glanced out of the window and saw Garnett and Margot Manley strolling along together. They were deep in conversation and the tall girl's shoulder was very little below his own. It seemed to Verity that he was looking happy; he flung back his head in the well-remembered way and laughed, and Margot smiled back at him with an unmistakable expression on her face.

Verity knew with a sinking of her heart that Margot Manley wanted Dr Rhodes, and who could resist such a glorious creature? She had also sensed on the few occasions that they had met that Margot did not like her.

It seemed a long and tedious journey to Mardale, but when she had reached the house and given all the details of the trip to London to the children and to Aunt Emma, she telephoned to Robert to say that she was coming out to the Works, and the whole business seemed to have been worth while as she saw the lines of strain ease from his face.

'Are you sure, Robert, that this will be enough?' she asked as she signed the cheque for eight hundred pounds.

'Look, Verity, there's no need for you to let me have any more that the six hundred I need to pay that bill. With that anxiety off my mind I can go right ahead.' His clever face was alight with enthusiasm. 'It's a good thing we managed to keep Father from coming to see how I was getting along,' he went on. 'If he knew how the orders have been coming in, wild horses wouldn't have kept him from getting back to work too soon. I'm sure the tide has turned for us now, Verity, and it's all thanks to you.'

He came over and kissed her awkwardly on the forehead. This meant a lot from Robert, who was not in any way demonstrative.

'I'll pay you back before they get back from Geneva,' he promised.

'I'm sure you will—but, Robert,' she said earnestly, 'if you can't manage it—I mean, if it's any help I can leave it invested in the business. I'd like anyway to have some share in it.'

'We'll have to let my father decide that,' he replied, and she cried out in anxiety that she did not want her father ever to know of the transaction.

'I tell him everything,' Robert answered gravely. 'And I have no doubt what his reaction will be. I'm in for a bit of a rough time when he does know.'

'I'll have to put this cheque into the bank tomorrow,' she said. 'It's after closing time now and I shall take it in first thing in the morning.'

'How did you manage to explain to your solicitor why you wanted to withdraw such a large amount?' he asked curiously.

'You forget, Robert, like everyone else. I'm twenty-one now and my own mistress.' And she smiled as she left him.

CHAPTER V

Everything was going well at the family house at Mardale. When Verity got home from London she found that the two children seemed to have accepted Aunt Emma, and in fact they seemed to have come to the conclusion that she was quite good fun when they got to know her better. Of course she was quite strict, and there was never any argument when she gave an order. Verity too began to like her very much indeed. She had a fund of common sense and in spite of the stern exterior she had a remarkable understanding of young people and was not censorious.

Verity had gone up to the school at the first opportunity to interview Miss Pargeter, and it had been arranged that when term began on the eighteenth of September, Verity would work three mornings a week taking the class of younger children in French lessons. She was glad of a few weeks' respite. It gave her a chance to be with Dinah and Simon and to get to know how their minds worked. She had not had a great deal of contact with small children before.

Letters came regularly from Mary in Geneva, and contained glowing accounts of the way in which John Gardner's health was improving, so that for the moment there did not seem to be any need to worry.

It was when Verity went into Leeds to collect the pearls from Mr Collier that she came into contact with Gerard again. She had decided some time ago that if he asked her out again she would refuse—not, she told herself, because in a way Garnett Rhodes had implied disapproval of the friendship, but—and then she could not really define her reasons. She was not therefore particularly pleased when, as she was leaving the shop, Gerard came towards her.

'Long time no see,' he greeted her in his flippant way.

'Good morning, Gerard,' she replied formally.

'I've been going to ring you to make a date for dinner. What about dining and dancing one evening this week?'

'I don't think I can manage it, Gerard,' she answered. 'I don't like to be out so much and leave Aunt Emma by herself. It's very kind of you, though, but—'

'I think it would be to your advantage to meet me.' He looked meaningly at the parcel she held in her hand.

Verity began to feel uneasy. There was something behind his remarks, she was sure.

'I can't imagine what you're talking about,' she said frostily. 'And if you don't mind I'd like to be getting along now. I shall miss my bus.'

'Thursday night at eight-thirty I'll pick you up.'

He stood between her and the door, and feeling that she should perhaps find out what was at the back of his mind she acquiesced reluctantly.

Mr Collier appeared at this moment and Gerard moved away as she hurried out of the shop.

All the way back to Mardale she thought about the curious remark Gerard had made, and then she dismissed the matter from her mind. She would go out with him this one last time. She wondered how on earth she had ever imagined that he was likeable. It was funny, she mused, that one's idea of people could change, and she found herself colouring slightly because in an unaccountable way her mind went back to the misunderstandings she seemed to have had with that other exasperating man, Garnett Rhodes. She resolved that the next time she met him he would not get any chance to make her feel small.

The day after her return Laura had telephoned and suggested that it would be a good idea on such a wonderful day to take the children out and give Aunt Emma a little time to herself. There was a lot of discussion when she told Dinah and Simon, and a slight difference of opinion, but eventually after Laura arrived and the picnic basket was ready it was a unanimous decision to go to Knaresborough and to visit the zoo there, and also the famous dropping well. It was a very happy party that set off and Aunt Emma, although she indomitably refused to admit she was tired, was sitting for once in the garden in a deck chair.

'Have a good time!' she called as they went out of the gates. 'And mind, now, no later than seven o'clock. I'll have your supper ready.'

'Do you know,' said Simon, 'I like my Aunt Emma, she's a good sort. Of course, I do miss Mummy and Daddy, but if we had to have anyone else Aunt Emma and Verity are the best.'

'I wonder if they'll bring a nice present back for us from Geneva?' Dinah was always the practical one of the pair.

'Look, there's the bus—run!' cried Laura, and soon they were ensconced at the back.

It was a lovely day and it was a tired but happy group which boarded the bus for the return journey. Dinah and Simon had revelled in the old town, the river, the Zoo and many delights, and were content to be silent now. In fact, from the heavy head

95

leaning against her Verity though Simon must be asleep. They would be home in good time and not incur Aunt Emma's wrath.

'I have enjoyed it, Verity.' Laura turned round from the seat in front. 'We've seen so little of you lately, but I know how you've helped Robert.'

'He promised—'

'I know, but I knew there was something seriously wrong and Robert and I have no secrets. It was wonderful of you, Verity, to come to the rescue in that way. I know you're used to having plenty of money, but some girls wouldn't have been so understanding.'

'You won't let anyone know?' said Verity anxiously. 'I don't want my father and Mary to have any kind of worry. This holiday is the first they've had since their marriage and it's doing Father so much good. I should hate anything to spoil it.'

'Of course it's safe with me.' Laura stopped then as they came into Mardale and it was time to rouse the two children.

'There've been two telephone calls for you, Verity,' said Aunt Emma. 'And both from young men.' Her eyes twinkled. 'Let's see.' She put on her spectacles and peered at the telephone pad. 'The first was from that young Gerard Manley. He told me to remind you that he would pick you up on Thursday.'

Verity thought that Laura looked a trifle uneasy and she hastily enquired who the other caller had been. Her heart leaped when she heard that it had been Garnett Rhodes.

'What did he want?' She could not keep the eagerness out of her voice.

96

'Well, funnily enough he wanted to call for you on Thursday night, but he seemed put out when I told him you already had a previous engagement.'

'Did you tell him who—?'

'Well, yes,' said Aunt Emma, puzzled. 'Shouldn't I have done? Do him good,' she chuckled. 'Nothing like a bit of competition, I think.'

Verity said goodbye to Laura, who wanted to hurry back to get Robert's supper, then she saw the children into bed with a heavy kind of feeling round her heart. What an unfortunate coincidence that Garnett Rhodes should have called to make a date for that particular evening! If only she had been in she could have put Gerard off with some excuse. It was no good, however. The arrangement would have to stand now, and Garnett would have the mistaken impression that she liked Gerard Manley. There was nothing she could do about it.

She could not help wondering what kind of evening he had planned. Then she determined that this really must be the last time she would go out with Gerard. She would try to end the friendship, though she went to bed with that uneasy feeling that he had some ulterior motive in asking her out on Thursday.

'You look wonderful,' said Aunt Emma with what for her was quite a soft and sentimental look. Verity was waiting for Gerard to call for her. Tonight she had chosen a dark green linen dress, high-necked and had chosen a dark green linen dress, high-necked and demure, and she was wearing pearls—not the real

'I'll be interested to meet this young man,' said Aunt Emma. 'He seemed very insistent that you shouldn't forget about the engagement for tonight.'

'Oh, Gerard is just a slight acquaintance. He took me out in London when Dr Rhodes had to attend a conference. That was on the day I first came home from Geneva.'

'I must admit it came as a surprise to me to find that John had another daughter. I can't understand why on earth he didn't get you back when he married again.'

'He had good reasons.' Verity spoke sharply; she was intensely loyal to her father, almost forgetting that this question had often puzzled her until she met him.

'I'm not wanting to pry, my dear.'

'No, of course not!' And Verity smiled with affection at the older woman. 'Oh, there's the door bell, it will be Gerard. Don't wait up for me, although I shall try to be in fairly early.'

As the girl went out Aunt Emma rose from her seat by the fire and went over to the window. She was not intending to pry, but she was curious to see the young man and wondered why Verity had not brought him in to be introduced.

She noticed that as Verity seated herself in the car and the fair-haired young man took his place beside her that there was no sparkle of anticipation on the girl's face, rather a resigned expression which did not augur well for the evening ahead. Verity glanced towards the house and Aunt Emma waved as the sports car drove away.

'We'll go to a quiet little place I know near Wetherby,' said Gerard.

Verity murmured some kind of assent and it seemed to strike Gerard that she was not as amiable as on former occasions.

'Cheer up,' he remarked. 'Has the old dragon

been getting you down? You didn't allow me to meet her, I noticed.'

' If you're talking about Aunt Emma,' Verity was coldly polite, ' she's a very fine woman and there's no reason for that kind of remark. I was pre-occupied, that's all.'

The rest of the journey took place in silence and it was not until they were seated in the very pleasant hotel dining room that Verity began to thaw out. Gerard exerted all his considerable charm and in spite of her misgivings she began to enjoy herself. It was later on the return journey, for Verity had insisted on being home early, that Gerard stopped the car.

' I think it's time we had a chat,' he suggested.

' What on earth do you mean?' she queried.

' About the pearls.'

Her hand flew to her throat and he reached out and touched the necklace lightly. She drew back, affronted.

' You can't fool me, you know. That's not the string you were wearing when we first met in London. They're a good imitation, but don't forget I'm in the jewellery trade. Besides—'

' Besides?' Again the note of question in her voice.

' I know it doesn't sound very noble of me, but I couldn't help hearing some of your conversation with Mr Collier.'

' You eavesdropped, you mean?'

Even Gerard flushed slightly at the contempt in her voice. There was silence for a while and at last he broke it.

' I gathered that you didn't want any hint of this little transaction to leak out.' And Verity realised with a feeling of relief that he had no idea of the real facts of the case. It would be as well, though, to find out what he had in mind, and she answered in a subdued voice.

'I would be upset, it's true, if anyone got to know that these are not the real pearls, but I can't understand what interest the matter has for you.'

'I'm quite prepared to keep quiet about them if you promise to do something for me.'

'I can't promise anything until I know what it is,' she said with some asperity. 'Don't be so tiresome, Gerard, making mysteries where there are none.'

'You're not really much of an heiress, are you?'

By now Verity found her temper was rising. It offended her sense of the fitness of things for this man to have so much knowledge about her affairs.

'I never made any claim to be an heiress,' she said with some difficulty, restraining herself from getting out of the car and leaving him. She must, however, find out what he was up to.

'Oh, it's not anything very difficult I want from you,' he said. 'Just keep out of Garnett Rhodes' way and let Margot have her chance.'

'Does your sister know you're doing this?' asked Verity coldly.

'Of course not,' he hedged. 'But I'm very fond of Margot, and things were practically settled between them until you arrived on the scene.'

Verity wondered if this was true, and then as she cast her mind back to the time when the doctor had shown that he disapproved of her friendship with Gerard, she remembered also that he had said 'Margot is different'. She felt a lump as heavy as lead rise in her throat and she could not reply.

'Just keep out of his way. You're very attractive, you know, and younger than Margot, and added to that there's the attraction of the money he thinks you possess.'

For some reason this hurt Verity more than any other remark he had made.

' I don't believe that of Dr Rhodes,' she flashed. ' Whatever else I've found about him, I know he's not a mercenary man.'

' You're attracted by him!' exclaimed Gerard, and then, ' You'll soon find someone else.' Abruptly he added: ' Is it a bargain?'

It didn't matter, she thought, whether he told anyone now about the pearls, but she did care that he should not let any of the facts about her money leak out to her family.

' How did you know I was not an heiress?' she queried.

' Simple. I just looked up your guardian's will at Somerset House. I wasn't able to do this until your solicitor obtained probate. Actually two thousand five hundred isn't to be sneezed at. A bit of a comedown, though, when you have been led to understand you would have a large income for life.'

' I never expected or thought about anything to do with money.' Her voice sounded small and meek and he smiled to himself with satisfaction, thinking that she had fallen for his trick.

' What do you suggest?' Her voice held a tinge of sarcasm, which quite escaped his notice. She might as well go along with his suggestions. Dr Rhodes had no interest in her, she was sure, and if he wanted Margot she did not intend to give any appearance of running after him. She felt a pang as she remembered the day they had driven to Harrogate; the evening spent in London after her parents' departure, and she shivered a little as she looked at the man who sat so blithe and unconcerned beside her.

'Just go out with me regularly,' he was saying.

'Good heavens, no!' She sounded so horrified that his eyes took on an ugly look.

'You didn't mind my company that night you arrived in London, and you've always been friendly enough before.'

He must have a hide as thick as a rhinoceros, she felt.

'I will come out with you, but not more than once a week. That should be enough to give people the idea that I'm not pursuing the doctor.' Once again her tone was ironic, but Gerard did not notice.

'That's settled, then,' he announced with satisfaction, and thought that Margot should be pleased. He was short of money again and he could get a little more from her every now and again if his scheme to draw Verity off succeeded.

He had no idea that all his plans were quite unnecessary, that far from holding any threat over her head, she was merely falling in with his ideas for her own convenience. True, he had left her with a heavy heart. She had not admitted even in her inmost thoughts that Dr Rhodes meant anything to her, but now it was no use trying to deceive herself. When she left Gerard and went into the house she found Aunt Emma waiting up for her.

'You look a bit peaky,' said that astute woman.

'I'm tired. I have enjoyed myself,' she went on defensively, 'but I wasn't in the mood for going out tonight.'

'Well, off to bed with you and I'll bring you a hot drink.' Aunt Emma bustled out into the kitchen and later she knocked on the bedroom door and came in with a steaming cup of Horlicks.

' You shouldn't have waited up for me.' Verity was finding the drink comforting and as she sat up in bed and sipped it she looked so very young that the older woman gave way to an unusual impulse, and sitting on the side of the bed she asked:

' Is there anything worrying you, my dear? You know you can confide in me. I'm good at keeping secrets.'

' No, no, really, it's just because I feel so tired tonight somehow. Truly, everything is fine.'

Aunt Emma was not to be taken in so easily, but being a wise woman she did not pursue the matter any further and took the cup and put out the light as she said, ' Good night.'

In the darkness, Verity folded her hands behind her head and went over the events of the evening. She smiled to herself a little as she thought about Gerard and his half-baked plot. If only he knew that he did not need to use any of these tactics.

She was not going to embarrass Garnett Rhodes, but her cheeks were wet with tears as she tossed and turned, unable to get to sleep. It was useless to try to keep her thoughts from turning to the remarks Gerard had made about his sister. Now she knew beyond any doubt that Dr Rhodes made any other man seem trivial and unimportant.

What was it, she wondered, which had caused her to change her mind towards him? On that first day at the airport, who could have imagined that she would find herself spending every unoccupied minute wondering about a man who, she was certain, did not give her more than a passing thought? And yet he had telephoned to ask her out. As she tossed and turned sleeplessly she came to a decision of a kind—

from now on, she said to herself firmly, no more time should be spent on vain surmising. At last she pulled the sheet over her head and slept.

Aunt Emma eyed her critically when she came down next morning.

'If you hadn't been home fairly early, I should have said you were suffering from too many late nights,' she remarked dryly.

'I'm quite all right.' Verity flushed and bent her head over the letter from Mary which had come that morning.

'Mary says Daddy looks so much better,' she said, in an effort to get off the subect of her own appearance. 'Funnily enough, he seems to have stopped worrying about getting home and is enjoying every minute of his leisure.'

'The best thing that has happened for years. I've told them time and time again that everyone needs a holiday, but you know your father—a very stubborn man. It wasn't fair to Mary either.'

'He was only trying to do the best for the family,' Verity flew to his defence, and Aunt Emma's strong features relaxed into a smile.

'When you get annoyed you are exactly like your mother.'

'Did you know her well?' Verity was eager. She had not liked to ask too many questions. It hardly seemed right when Mary was around, although she knew that Mary and her own mother, Isobel, had been friends.

'Yes, I knew her, and you are very like her in many ways, but she was a beauty, of course.'

At this remark Verity was forced to laugh, and as Aunt Emma rose purposefully to get on with the daily routine, she decided to leave the matter for the time being. She longed to know more about that shadowy personality, but perhaps some day when he was home her father might enlighten her, and if not it was sufficient to know that Isobel seemed to have been generally beloved.

'Where are the children?' she asked, as she realised that they must have finished their breakfast early.

'They're down in the garden with the two boys from next door,' said Aunt Emma. 'Thank goodness it's school next week. They have far too long holidays, to my mind.'

The reminder that school was due to start next Tuesday made Verity conscious that she also was to start work. She felt a little sense of unease as she contemplated the task of trying to impart a knowledge of French to a group of small but no doubt critical children. She decided that for the next few days she must get out some of her books and study a little. Then her spirits rose as she remembered that her job was to be part-time only. She would have to try to keep one step ahead of her class.

It was the following week that Gerard telephoned again and suggested that he should take Verity out to dinner. Reluctantly she agreed, determined that when they returned, after the evening out, she would tell him that he could go ahead and talk about the pearls; about the fact that she was not an heiress.

If she were not mistaken in her judgement of him, he would crumple. Robert was a forceful young-man and she had a suspicion that Gerard was a typical bully where women were concerned, but was no match for anyone in physical courage.

She was tired. Her first week at the school had passed off well. The work was not difficult, but there had been the slight feeling of strain which attends any new venture. She was determined also to keep up with the classes in typing and shorthand which she had started and to fit herself for some kind of secretarial work when Mademoiselle Giravd returned to the school.

Aunt Emma gave a disapproving sniff when she heard the ring at the door and this time she came out to inspect Verity's escort. From the expression on her face it seemed she was not very favourably impressed.

'We'll dine at that little place near Harrogate again,' said Gerard, 'and then I have a little surprise for you.'

'And I have one for you,' Verity murmured.

'What did you say?'

'Oh, nothing, I'll tell you later.'

It was nearly ten o'clock when they left the hotel and Gerard swung the car in an unfamiliar direction.

'Where are you going?' Verity asked. 'I wanted to be home early tonight.'

'You are a little spoilsport, aren't you? Do you know when we first met I could have sworn you liked a good time.'

'Seriously, Gerard, I want to go home now, and also I want to talk to you.'

'Too late,' he said blithely. 'We're here,' and he drove through the large wrought iron gates and up a long tree-shaded drive. They stopped in front of a wide flight of stone steps leading to a wide door with a Georgian fanlight. 'I'm taking you to meet some friends of mine.'

After parking the car behind half a dozen others,

he led her up the wide steps. There was a chorus of greetings as they went into the large brightly lit hall. Verity blinked in the glare and acknowledged the introductions, not really taking in the names. A maid led her upstairs to leave her wrap and then she came down and found Gerard waiting impatiently.

' I'm joining one of the card games,' he said. ' And by the way, can you lend me a fiver? I've come out without much money.'

As she searched in her tiny evening bag, Verity realised that this habit of borrowing was becoming pretty frequent, and not yet had Gerard offered to refund any of the sums he had got from her on one pretext or another.

' I've only got three pounds,' she answered, and he frowned, but almost grabbed it from her hand before he turned to leave her.

' Gerard!' she spoke sharply. ' I don't want to be late home. You promised. And what am I supposed to do?'

' Go into the back room, there's dancing there. You'll find no difficulty in getting to know everyone, they're a friendly crowd.'

As she stood rather timidly in the doorway and listened to the noisy record which was being played, and surveyed the crowd of youngsters who were moving in time to the beat, she looked longingly for some place to take refuge. On the way home she would tell Gerard finally that he could tell the whole world about her affairs. She had begun to dislike him more than she could possibly have imagined.

' Come on, kid!'

Before she could collect her thoughts she was drawn into the centre of the dancers and found that her partner was a rather engaging-looking youth with a shock of long blond hair. He looked clean enough and was reasonably polite. When the record finished and there was a lull, he took her to a seat by the window and began to chat. She found his conversation amusing but immature, and after some little time she felt restless and tried to excuse herself. She would go to Gerard and ask to be taken home.

'Rubbish!' said her companion. 'Relax and enjoy yourself. Here, have a cigarette, nothing like it for soothing the nerves.'

Verity was not an habitual smoker, but she did occasionally have one on social occasions, and, unsuspectingly, she took one from the case. It was only when she put it to her lips and inhaled the first puff that she felt that there was something wrong, and looked at the cigarette closely.

'What's this?' she queried.

'Go on, finish it—you'll like it.'

But Verity flung the offending cigarette on to the floor and stamped on it, then, pushing the boy to one side, ran out of the room. She went swiftly across the hall to the card room and broke abruptly into the game. Gerard glanced up impatiently; he was intent and he was obviously having a winning streak.

'Take me home, now, Gerard!' she burst out.

The other players looked at her curiously and began to smile, and Gerard's face suffused with anger.

'Oh, go and get lost!' he snapped, and this time it was Verity who was angry. Leaving with as much dignity as she could muster, she made her way up to the room where she had left her mink stole.

As she came down the wide staircase, she met the maid who had shown her in and asked:

'Where is this place?'

The woman looked at her in some surprise, but answered civilly:

'This is Red Gables, madam, the home of Mr and Mrs Redgrave.'

'How far is it from Mardale?'

'About two miles.'

'Thank you. If Mr Manley is asking about me will you tell him that I've been called away?'

The woman held open the wide oak door, and Verity swept out. It was when she got outside that her predicament hit her with full force. She looked down at her flimsy sandals. Fortunately, the heels were not too high, but the evening had turned chilly and the thin dress and light stole were not much protection. She was going to look rather absurd walking along the country roads in this attire. However, it was not too far and, setting her determined little chin, she hurried off down the long drive. As she passed Gerard's flamboyant sports car she paused, regretting for the first time that she had not done as Laura had advised and taken her driving test. She could quite well have driven the car, but it would be folly to risk being stopped. She could not help thinking that it would serve Gerard right if he were to come out and find it gone.

She determined to keep well into the side of the road and take cover if she heard any traffic approaching. It was pretty quiet at the moment. Verity glanced at her tiny watch, and found it was after midnight. She remembered too late that she had no idea in which direction she should be going and felt a sharp pang of annoyance. She could have asked the maid at the house.

Heavy rain had begun to fall. She had vaguely remembered that as they entered the drive they had come in from the right-hand fork of the road, so she proceeded in this direction. Her dress was bedraggled and soaked, and the wet fur did nothing to keep her warm. Suddenly she heard the hum of the engine of a high-power car and started to run to gain the shelter of a clump of trees overhanging the hedge, but her foot caught on a large stone and she fell sprawling. Somehow she got to her feet, but her right ankle twisted under her, and she was vainly trying to hobble to the trees when the large car swept round the corner. It went past her and she breathed a premature sigh of relief because immediately it stopped and the door opened.

She stared up into the dark face of the one man she would not have chosen to be her rescuer.

'What on earth do you think you're doing?' demanded Dr Rhodes, his dark brows drawn together in the familiar disapproving way.

'I've hurt my foot,' Verity said feebly.

He opened the nearside door of the car and picked her up and put her on the seat. Without a word he got in beside her and then lifting her foot his strong fingers probed and twisted it gently. She winced with pain, but he said as he reached for his bag from the rear seat:

'It's only a slight sprain. I'll strap it up.' He proceeded to do so deftly and she sighed with relief.

'You're soaked to the skin,' he said angrily. 'I'd better get you home as quickly as possible, and meanwhile, as we go, I'd like some explanations.'

Reluctantly she told him the gist of the story, trying to gloss over Gerard's refusal to bring her home, but she could tell by the look on his face that he was not deceived.

'What made you so anxious to leave?' he asked.

' I don't really know. There was something funny about those dancers, and I didn't like that cigarette the boy offered me.'

With a grinding of brakes the big car stopped. He pulled her towards him, his face almost touching hers, and his hands gripped her shoulders so tightly that it hurt.

' Do you know, you silly little idiot, that was marijuana! You smoked it—I can smell it on your breath.'

' I didn't, I didn't,' she protested. ' He lit it for me, but I thought it was funny and threw it away.'

He started up the car again. ' I'll get you home now and I'll have a word with that young man in the morning!'

They drove the rest of the short journey in silence and when he stopped outside the house at Mardale she spoke in a low voice.

' Dr Rhodes, please don't say anything to Gerard about this. There's no harm done and I can assure you I won't be going out with him again. You were right about him, it was just that I—'

' You don't like being dictated to by someone who has no right to interfere with your affairs.' He spoke dryly.

She sighed wearily and, with an exclamation, he came round to open the door for her. Before she could protest he had gathered her up in his arms and taken her up the steps to the front door. He put her down carefully, but she still felt the pain in her ankle and leaned against him, fumbling with the catch of her bag. She found the key and he took it from her, and opening the door he carried her through and into the sitting room. He switched on the lamp by the settee and put on the electric fire.

'You need to get out of those things as quickly as possible,' he said. 'And have a hot drink and a bath before you get into bed.'

'I'll manage now, thank you very much, and you won't—'

'I'll not take any action this time,' he answered.

There was a noise behind him and he swung round to see Aunt Emma, majestic in a mannish dressing gown, her iron grey hair confined in a net. She showed no sign of surprise that Verity should have gone out with one young man and come back with another.

'Miss Gardner has sprained her ankle slightly and I've bandaged it for her. It was fortunate that I was able to give her a lift home. She is, however, very wet, but then,' and he turned the full force of that charming smile, which so illuminated his face, towards the older woman, 'I'm sure I can leave her safely in your capable hands.'

As Aunt Emma obediently went to run the bath, Garnett looked at the bedraggled girl. In spite of her wet hair and untidy appearance she had a wistful charm which tugged at his heart. A great surge of anger rose up inside him as he blessed the night call which had brought him to her assistance.

'I'll go now,' he said, and Verity raised her head, the huge golden eyes shadowed.

'Thank you, Dr Rhodes. I've been very foolish, I admit, but please, please, don't do anything about Gerard. I'll deal with him myself.'

'Haven't we known each other long enough,' he said almost angrily, 'to drop the formality? I have a christian name.'

'I'm sorry,' she stammered. 'It's only—'

'I suppose I seem like Methuselah to you?'

Then he came over to the settee and took a last look at the injured ankle.

'You'll be able to hobble about on that tomorrow.' He bent and dropped a gentle kiss on her cheek before turning to go.

He still thinks of me as a child, Verity thought resentfully, but as she remembered the events of the evening, common sense came to her aid and she was able to smile gratefully as Aunt Emma came back.

'A hot bath and then to bed, young woman, and I'll bring you a drink.'

As Verity sat up in bed with her hands clasped round the comforting warmth of the beaker of hot milk, she remembered the security she had felt as Garnett carried her indoors, the strength of the arms which had held her and the steady pounding of his heart beneath her ear.

'That's quite a man!' Aunt Emma's deep voice broke in on her thoughts and as she drowsed, the words seemed to throb in the distance. 'Quite a man, quite a man!'

CHAPTER VI

There was a phone call from Gerard next morning
and even more disturbing was the paragraph in the
daily paper which told of a raid by the police on the
club known as Red Gables—not because of the
gambling club but because the police had had a tip
that there was some evidence of drug-taking among
the younger members of the club. Verity felt herself
turn pale as she read it. What an escape! She
made short work of Gerard's apologies and firmly
refused to see him any more.

' You can do and say what you like,' she told him.
' If I go to my brother Robert he'll soon deal with
you.'

' I've said I was sorry.'

If she had not been so furious it would have been
almost laughable to contemplate the way in which he
managed to hide his head in the sand like an ostrich
when trouble threatened.

' Oh well, it doesn't matter now. Margot is going
to get what she wants without any help from me.'

With this cryptic remark he rang off, leaving
Verity with the unpalatable feeling that the man she
loved had come to some kind of decision about
Margot, and that the best thing she could do would
be to forget him. Difficult, as he was a personal
friend of her family and she must come in contact
with him from time to time. The events of the previous night would have confirmed his original opinion
of her.

He would think of her forever as a feather-brained,
spoilt little rich girl. That first unfortunate

encounter at the airport had started the whole thing. If she could have met him later, when she had become established as a daughter of the house, things might—no use dreaming, and she bent all her energies on her new work at the school. It was not too difficult. The children were not critical, and soon she found that she was enjoying her morning sessions, and she was working hard at the business college, determined to fit herself for some kind of career.

John and Mary had been away for two months and now were talking of their return to Mardale. It would be quite a wrench, Mary wrote, to leave the flat, the lake, and all the lazy luxurious life they had been living, but they could hardly wait to be with the family again, and for her part Verity longed for their return. Aunt Emma was a tower of strength and the children a constant delight, but somehow she had not been able to get near to Sara. The older girl came home from the hospital to sleep, but she was preoccupied with plans for her marriage, and although she was perfectly polite to Verity there was no bond between them.

Verity arrived home one lunch time to find Aunt Emma in what, for her, was a state of agitation.

' I'm so glad you're back,' she cried. ' Matron has been on the telephone and she's sending Sara home by taxi. She's not at all well and Matron suggests we get the doctor in as soon as she arrives.

' Oh, it's nothing very serious,' she hurried on as she saw Verity's alarmed expression. ' Matron said she would have kept Sara in the sick bay at the hospital, but they're having rather a bad patch at the moment and it's pretty full. I said we would be able to manage her at home.'

' Of course. I'll just see to her bedroom, and you can let Dr Elliot know.'

It was about twenty minutes later when the taxi arrived. Sara looked very flushed and seemed to have difficulty in talking.

' It's only a sore throat,' she croaked.

They soon had her tucked up in bed and Aunt Emma departed for the kitchen to make some soothing drinks. Dr Elliot, who arrived after lunch, examined Sara and pronounced that she had a severe infection.

' See that the two youngsters don't go into her room,' he advised. ' Dinah has had a lot of bother with her tonsils and we don't want her to be exposed in any way.'

' We'll see to it,' Verity replied. ' Do you think we should let my father and Mary know?'

' Not necessary. She should be all right in a few days and it would be a pity to spoil the rest of their stay. I know Mary, she would insist on taking the next plane home. What about your teaching?' he asked.

' It's only three mornings a week, and I can manage if Verity gives me a hand when she's at home,' Aunt Emma declared.

For the first couple of days things went smoothly. Sara had a very nasty attack and was quite poorly. Aunt Emma insisted on attending to her herself as she did not want anyone else to risk being infected. It was on the third day that she slipped as she was carrying down the breakfast tray. Verity heard the crash and raced for the hall to find the two children looking very upset, and trying to help Aunt Emma to her feet.

' Don't move for a minute until we see whether

you've done any damage,' Verity observed. ' You two go down to the gate, Mr Wilson will be waiting to pick you up.'

It was obvious as soon as the older woman tried to rise that there was something wrong with her right leg and after placing the cushion behind her head and covering her with a rug, Verity raced to the telephone. The receptionist said that one of the doctors would be round as soon as possible, and when Verity got back to the victim she found that Sara had put on her dressing gown and come down the stairs. She was still far from well, and shaky, so that when Verity sharply ordered her back to bed she was glad to return upstairs.

Verity was sitting on the bottom step supporting the injured woman when the door bell rang and the door opened, and so perturbed was she about the accident that it did not really register that it was not Dr Elliot who had come but Garnett Rhodes. She had not seen him since that night when he had brought her home. With his usual efficiency the leg was examined and an ambulance summoned. Verity could not leave Sara so that she was glad that there was a nurse in attendance.

Garnett Rhodes watched the vehicle turn out of the gate and then he came back into the house.

' I'll take a look at Sara now I'm here,' he said. ' It will save Dr Elliot a visit.'

He ran upstairs and Verity rang Miss Pargeter to explain that she would not be able to get into school that morning, in fact that, until she knew how serious the injury to Aunt Emma was, she might not be able to come for some time. To her surprise Miss Pargeter seemed quite relieved and after expressing her regret about the accident, she remarked:

'It's really quite providential, but I've had a letter from Mademoiselle Giravd. Owing to the death of her mother, she is anxious to return to the school as soon as possible. I was wondering how to approach you about the matter, but now I should imagine you would perhaps be glad to be relieved of the post. Not,' she added hastily, ' that we shall not be sorry to lose you. You've done a splendid job with the children, but I know that you are not really in need of work, while Mademoiselle Giravd is dependent on her earnings.'

Verity hastily agreed as she heard the doctor running down the stairs.

'Sara isn't too well yet,' he remarked. ' She'll need a good long rest. What a pity Aunt Emma has had this mishap.'

'Do you think she'll have to stay in hospital?' Verity sounded worried because she had a vision of the difficulties of looking after the home and Sara and trying to fit in visits to Aunt Emma.

'I don't think so. Even if the ankle is fractured they'll probably keep her in for the night and then send her home with the leg in plaster. What's the matter?' He sounded impatient. ' Are you afraid you won't have so much time for gadding about?'

If it had not been for the sudden flash of anger which came to her rescue, Verity could have burst into tears.

'I'm just considering ways and means,' she replied coldly.

He glanced at his watch, and after giving a few instructions about Sara he said: ' I'll ring back later. I have an appointment at the hospital this morning and should be able to find out about your aunt.'

He left without a backward glance and Verity

stood for a minute staring after the back of the grey car before she ran upstairs to attend to Sara.

As she made the bed and her sister sat wrapped in the eiderdown in the armchair, the two girls chatted.

' I do wish I hadn't got this beastly throat,' sighed Sara. ' Here I am, a trained nurse, and not able to help when an emergency arises.'

' Don't worry about a thing. I'll be able to manage.' Verity spoke with an air of quiet assurance and Sara looked at her curiously.

' There'll be an awful lot to do. I know Mrs Tennant comes in for the housework, but there'll be all the running about and cooking, and the children take a lot of watching.'

' Look, Sara, will you stop treating me like a child? Let me try for a few days and then, if you have any criticism of my ability to make, you can do so!' and Verity marched out of the room for once thoroughly fed up with this myth which had arisen through no fault of hers, that she was some kind of delicate flower to be shielded from the least hint of hardship.

She swept round the house like a tornado. Mrs Tennant arrived at ten o'clock and found Verity very much on top.

' My word, miss,' she said admiringly as she looked at the neatly set tray for Sara's elevenses, and surveyed the preparations already under way for the lunch, ' I'd no idea you could cook!'

' Will you take this up at eleven for Miss Sara?' Verity answered, still in no mood to hear any more comments on her ability to work.

Garnett Rhodes telephoned before lunch and, as he had thought, the fracture was not a bad one. Aunt Emma would be sent home in the morning.

'How are you going to manage?' he queried. 'Don't you think you should ask Laura to come over for a few days to take charge?'

With a note in her voice which made the man at the other end of the telephone hold the receiver away from his ear with a look of astonishment, Verity snapped:

'If I need any assistance from Laura, I'm quite capable of making up my own mind whether to ask for it. Thank you for your message, it was kind of you to let me know—and now, if you don't mind, I'm too busy to indulge in a long conversation.' She put down the receiver with a bang and then proceeded to the kitchen where she sipped a cup of coffee and made out her plan of campaign.

Aunt Emma came back next day and it was evident, although she made light of her injury, that the incident had shaken her more than she was prepared to admit. She had a plaster on her leg from foot to knee and was warned that she must not walk on it until she was allowed a walking plaster. She was quite content to sit in the living room and mend socks, and, what was more, she made no attempt to advise or direct Verity. Her keen eyes had noted that everything seemed to be running smoothly, so she sat back and accepted the situation. Dinah and Simon were being very helpful. They loved to run errands and when Aunt Emma began to hobble about they were highly amused by the sight of her trying to manipulate the ' pot leg '.

'I really ought to be getting back to work.' Sara was sitting in the kitchen watching Verity baking one of her batches of cakes. 'I do think it's silly to be sitting around uselessly. I feel fine now.'

'Don't be in too much of a hurry,' advised Verity.

'Dr Elliot said you were overworked when you picked up that nasty throat infection. They'll be managing quite well without you for a little while longer. It's a big help to me, too, for you to be able to keep an eye on the children and Aunt Emma. I'm so afraid she'll start wanting to work before that ankle is strong enough.'

'Oh, by the way,' said Sara, 'I forgot to tell you, Margot Manley is coming in every day to give Aunt Emma some physiotherapy now that the plaster is coming off. Dr Rhodes thought it would be better than taking her into Leeds for treatment. Isn't it kind of him? I do think he's the most attractive man, except for Michael, of course.'

'When does Miss Manley begin the treatment?' Verity appeared to be busy removing a tray of tarts from the Aga oven, but she listened intently to the reply.

'Oh, tomorrow, I think. I wonder if she'll manage to get Garnett Rhodes?'

'What a horrible way of putting it!' Verity said sharply.

'It's been a matter for conjecture at the hospital for a long time now. They've certainly been seen around and he doesn't seem to be interested in anyone else. Is anything the matter, Verity?' she finished. 'You look tired.'

'No, no, it's nothing. I've been leaning over this hot stove. I'll open the window,' and Verity went to take a few gulps of fresh air. The suffocating sense of despair which Sara's innocent chatter had aroused in her brought back all the painful memories she had tried to push to the back of her mind.

'Verity!' Sara's voice sounded diffident as she came over to stand by the other girl. 'I do want to thank you for all you've done for me since I've been ill. You know,' she continued with a rush, ' I don't think I've been at all fair to you. It's only since I've been at home and had time to think that I realise how lonely you must have felt.'

Verity turned, her face radiant with joy. It had worried her that of all the family, Sara had seemed the least interested in her.

' I do feel now,' Sara went on earnestly, ' that you are my sister, and it's a good feeling. I love little Dinah, of course, but it's going to be wonderful to have someone near to my own age.'

She gave Verity a sudden hug and then almost ran from the room.

Verity was roused from the happy reverie in which she was indulging by the realisation that if lunch was to be ready on time she would have to keep her mind on her work, but she sang to herself and the forlorn feeling which had overtaken her earlier was pushed into the background of her thoughts.

Dr Rhodes brought Margot Manley the following day to see Aunt Emma and to arrange the times for treatment. He also pronounced Sara fit for work on the following Monday.

Margot usually came during the morning and it was surprising how many times Dr Rhodes arrived at this time to see the invalid. Verity thought resentfully, as she carried in a tray of coffee and some of her dainty cakes each morning, that there was a faintly malicious look on Margot's face. The doctor would accept his cup from Verity and then continue his conversation without appearing to notice her more than he would have done a piece of furniture.

Margot was always vivacious and gay and Aunt

Emma would look from one to the other with her shrewd gaze. One morning she upset her coffee and Dr Rhodes, after making sure that none had splashed on to her, said:

'I'll get a cloth and another cup for you. Don't worry, I know my way about.'

Margot did not look too pleased, but she was busy packing her equipment as she had another appointment and would have to hurry away.

The old house was comfortable and roomy, if slightly old-fashioned in design, but the kitchen was as up-to-date and modern as it could possibly be. John Gardner said that it was no advertisement of his factory if his own kitchen was not something of a showpiece.

Verity was kneeling down in front of the Aga when the doctor walked in. A lock of hair had fallen over her face, which was flushed, and she was surveying the joint in an absorbed manner. Although he had entered so silently she must have felt his presence and the tin slipped from her hand. She caught it deftly, but a little of the boiling fat splashed over her fingers and she gave a slight squeak of pain.

'Goodness, you did startle me!' she exclaimed as she hastily wiped the fat from her hand with a piece of kitchen paper.

'Let me look.' His hand was firm as he grasped her wrist and looked at the fingers.

'No damage done,' he pronounced. 'This is a pleasant kitchen,' he continued, looking round at the cupboards and fitted surfaces, the usual decorations and the light streaming through the large window. 'I've spilt Aunt Emma's coffee, is there any chance of another cup for her?'

'I'll just heat some up,' and Verity turned thankfully to get out of the gaze of those penetrating eyes.

'You seem to be coping very well,' was his next remark.

For some reason this seemingly innocent comment roused Verity to her usual state of combined fascination and anger whenever Garnett Rhodes was about.

If she had taken the trouble to look at him she would have seen that the strong dark face was looking indulgent and more approachable. It was unfortunate that when she did glance in his direction, as she handed him the tray with the fresh coffee, his eyes once more held that quizzical, rather mocking expression.

After he had gone out of the kitchen she heard the sound of Margot's car driving away and breathed a sigh of relief. One of them at a time was enough to contend with.

She had regained her composure and was busily putting the finishing touches to the rather special cold sweet which she had prepared for the evening meal, when the doctor appeared again.

'I've been talking to Aunt Emma,' he said, 'and she agrees with me that you're beginning to look tired. We can't have you cracking up at this stage. Mary would insist on coming straight back and it's important that they take the full length of time away.'

He's not bothered about me at all, she felt resentfully, but at his next words, in spite of herself, her heart beat more rapidly as he went on:

'I've rung Laura and she'll come over for the rest of the day, and you're to take a break.'

'But—' she began.

'Don't argue. As it happens I have to go out to Ripon to see my father. I'll pick you up at half past two.'

Without giving her any chance to remonstrate or refuse he was gone, and Verity left the lunch for a minute and went in to see Aunt Emma.

' Of all the bossy, interfering—' she began, but was interrupted.

' I like a man who knows his mind, and he's quite right. How long is it since you went out, even to the shops? A breath of country air will do you the world of good.'

' I could quite well have gone out for a walk by myself,' Verity protested, but somewhat feebly.

She served and cleared away lunch in quick time and Laura arrived promptly.

' You know, you should have asked me before,' she said. ' You're beginning to look tired out. I don't know what Mummy and Daddy will say if they come back to find you a wreck.'

' Are you sure it's convenient?'

' Of course. I hadn't anything on this afternoon and I've told Robert to come out here for dinner.'

' It's all ready,' Verity told her, ' something cold with salad, and I've made a special sweet.'

' It all looks absolutely delicious. You must give me the recipe some time. Where on earth did you learn to cook like this?'

' Our old cook in Geneva taught me a lot—and besides,' said Verity shyly, ' I took the Cordon Bleu course when we were in Paris for a few months.'

' You are a dark horse!' Then Laura shooed her upstairs to get ready. ' Better not keep Garnett waiting, he's rather an impatient type.'

' So I've noticed,' said Verity dryly.

' You're favoured, though. I don't remember anyone being taken to his home before. Not even

Margot,' Laura said with a faint touch of malice in her voice.

' It's just his professional eye which thinks I look tired and need a change.'

' He's right, of course, you ought to have let me help a little more,' Laura reproached.

' Oh, Laura, I didn't mean to keep you out. It was just that I wanted to show people that I was some use after all.'

' You've certainly made quite sure that no one thinks of you as a helpless little rich girl,' chuckled Laura. ' Even though the rich part may be true.'

' I'd better get ready on time and not keep that autocrat waiting.' And Verity ran upstairs, determined to keep off the subject of her circumstances.

He seemed far from autocratic, though, when at last they were speeding along the roads towards Ripon. He was preoccupied, and for a long time they had no exchange of conversation.

At last, seeming to realise that he was neglecting his passenger, he asked her if she liked what she had seen of Yorkshire.

' I haven't of course had much opportunity of visiting many of the places of interest yet,' she answered.

' I think you'll find Ripon a pleasant old city and if we have time before we reach my father's house— he's not expecting me until four—we'll have a look at the Cathedral. It will be market day, being Thursday, so you should find it of particular interest to see the old place today.'

They caught a glimpse of the busy market stalls as they passed down the side street, up the hill, and parked the big car down by the side of the Cathedral.

' I have almost,' he remarked, ' more affection for

this Cathedral than for York Minster, though of course that's one of the outstanding glories of our county. I used to sing in the choir here.'

As they entered the beautiful building and she listened to him explaining the points of interest, she found herself picturing him as a small boy; especially when they came to the curiously carved choir stalls and he showed her the book, ancient but well preserved, which gave the history of the carvings. They spent a long time there and she felt a kind of peace steal into her heart, and she felt regret when finally he decreed that they must go.

'I shall always remember this first glimpse of an English cathedral,' she thanked him shyly.

Looking down at her, he said: 'There are many more wonders in this county of ours—the abbeys, and York itself is one of the wonders of the world. I'll—' and then he left whatever it had been unsaid.

His father was a tall grey-haired, rather stooped and scholarly looking clergyman, and he welcomed Verity warmly.

She enjoyed the tea and the talk and sensed the great affection which lay between the two men. She gathered that Garnett was his only son, that his wife had died some years ago and that he was well looked after by a middle-aged housekeeper.

Mr Rhodes and Verity got on well from the moment they met, and after tea, a real Yorkshire meal with table groaning with scones, cakes, curd tarts and other delicacies, he showed her round his precious library. Garnett left them together as he had calls to make on old friends and it was fairly late when he returned. He found the two of them still chatting happily.

'Sorry to break up the party, but we'd better be

getting back to Mardale and I thought,' he turned to his father, ' that we would stop in the market place. It might interest Verity to hear the Wakeman.'

The elderly housekeeper came out to the door with them and remarked: ' You must come again, miss, quite cheered the Rector up. Of course, I know the doctor hasn't much time for visiting, he works too hard, I tell him, but then,' and she looked up at him fondly, ' he always was one for putting duty first.'

They drove into the now almost deserted market square and sat waiting in the car. At nine precisely the picturesque figure of the Wakeman appeared outside the town hall and Verity watched, and listened fascinated, as he blew his horn.

As they left the city, she turned to her companion and said a little shyly:

' Thank you for bringing me out this afternoon. It's been such a treat, and particularly meeting your father. He is a most interesting man.'

' I'm glad you liked him. I am afraid I don't have time to see as much of him as I would like, but he understands.'

' Are you the only one?' she asked.

' No, I have a sister. She's several years older than I am, and she is now in Nigeria with her husband and the three children. They're due home next year on leave. It's a pity for my father that they're so far away, but he's looking forward to see-ing them, and especially the youngest grandchild, who was born out there.'

They were now approaching Mardale and she wondered if he would just deposit her at the door in his usual way, but this time he had evidently decided to come in and accompanied her to the living room.

Aunt Emma was by herself and she looked keenly

at Verity, remarking with satisfaction,

'That's better. You look a different person now. Time you had a change of scene.'

'I'll make some coffee,' said Verity, escaping to the kitchen.

When she came back, Sara and Michael had arrived and were bubbling over with excitement. They had seen the ideal house and were in the thick of planning for an early wedding. The conversation was about mortgages, bridesmaids, etc., and Verity had never seen her sister so excited.

It was late when Garnett Rhodes unfolded his long length reluctantly from the comfortable depths of his chair.

'I'll have to be going, I'm on surgery duty tomorrow,' he declared.

'See Dr Rhodes out, Verity,' commanded Aunt Emma. 'And by the way, young man,' she continued, 'don't you think it's high time I began to walk about a bit more and stop all this fancy physiotherapy, as you call it?'

'Just a bit longer,' he smiled as he looked down at her. 'Miss Manley has done a good job, but you must be careful for a while yet.'

At this moment the telephone rang and Sara went to answer it. She seemed to be excited as she talked. Verity had just reached the front door with Garnett when Sara rushed out of the living room.

'That was Robert. He's been working late tonight at the factory and he's just had a phone call from Dad. They're coming home on Thursday. Robert says Father is absolutely fit again now. He's seen the doctor whom Garnett recommended and there's no reason why he shouldn't come back to work straight away. Robert said Mummy sounded so excited too. She's loved Geneva but is longing to see us all, and I'm afraid she's a little bit annoyed because we never let her know earlier about Aunt Emma. She sends her special love to you, Verity. I wrote and told her how marvellously you'd coped with things.'

After all the exclaiming and chatter Verity let Garnett out, and went to the doorstep with him.

She was glad of course that her parents were returning and although, as Sara had said, she had coped admirably, she had begun to feel a slight sense of strain lately, and she could not help feeling a little nervous at her father's reactions when he found out about that wretched loan. She knew Robert too well by now to believe that he would keep the matter a secret.

Would her father be angry with Robert? She did so want this to be a happy homecoming and she was not afraid for her own sake, but Robert had worked hard to keep the business going and she dreaded him having to face his father's wrath.

She had almost forgotten her companion until she heard his deep voice.

'What is it, Verity?'

'What do you mean?' she stammered.

'There's something wrong, isn't there? Aren't you glad your people are coming home?'

She sighed, and he said swiftly:

'If you're in any kind of trouble, you know you can count on me. Is it anything to do with that young scoundrel Manley? You haven't—?'

'I promised I wouldn't see him again.' Her voice was low. 'No, Doctor—I mean Garnett, I can't tell you why I'm worried, but believe me it's nothing very serious. I shall be delighted to see my parents again, of course. I have hardly had time to get to know them.'

He held her shoulders in that firm yet gentle grip.

' You don't need me to remind you that I want to be your friend,' he said, and it took her all her time not to cry out, ' It's not your friendship that I need!'

' Thank you, I know that, Garnett,' she replied. ' And I hope that I am yours.'

He stood looking at her in the dim light, a rather puzzled look on his face, then he took her in his arms and kissed her gently.

She buried her face against his tweed jacket and the tears came. He took out a large handkerchief and wiped them gently away.

' I'll get Dr Elliot to have a look at you,' he said. ' You're obviously suffering from overwork.'

She gave a sudden nervous giggle with reaction at this prosaic remark and he drew back, his dark face stern once more.

' Good night,' he said, and turned, and the grey car roared away down the drive leaving her to think that she always managed to end the evening on a wrong note. She went back to the others to join in the talk, after first making sure by a glance in the hall mirror that the signs of tears did not seem to show. She thought Aunt Emma was not deceived, but she did not say anything until at last she shooed them all off to bed.

' If they're coming home on Saturday there'll be a lot to see to, and you, young lady, need to get some sleep!'

But sleep seemed far away as Verity tossed and turned all night, and by the morning it was obvious that she could not get out of bed. Sara could not stay away from the hospital, so Laura promised to be over as soon as possible, and Aunt Emma had made up her mind to phone for the doctor and was considerably surprised when Dr Elliot appeared as if by magic before she had time to make the necessary call.

'Just a severe attack of migraine,' he pronounced. 'She'll be over it by tomorrow. Has anything been upsetting her? I came over because Garnett left a message for me to have a look at her. It was on the list for this morning.'

'Never thought of coming himself, I suppose?' said Aunt Emma caustically.

Dr Elliot looked a bit surprised.

'Well, it is his surgery. How's the leg doing?'

'It's quite better now, I'm sure, without all this nonsense about having treatment all the time. That Miss Manley is coming this morning and I hope to goodness it will be for the last time. Oh, I'm not saying anything about her work, she's done a good job on my leg, but—'

'Well, I'll have to be going,' said Dr Elliot. 'I've got a long round to do, and just keep Verity quiet for today. I've left some tablets. I expect the excitement of the news about John and Mary coming back was the cause of the attack.'

'I wonder, I wonder,' said Aunt Emma to herself rather cryptically as he left.

CHAPTER VII

Verity soon recovered from the unfortunate attack of migraine. Dr Elliot, in his kindly way, read her a lecture on the folly of trying to do more than one pair of hands was able to accomplish Verity acquiesced meekly enough, although her mind was already busy with plans for the return of her parents on the Thursday. It left only two days in which to prepare a welcome, and she went into conference with Mrs Tennant, who polished and cleaned with fresh zeal.

'You know,' said Sara, when she was home on one of her shifts off from the hospital, 'Mummy isn't going to take a bit of notice how the house looks. Thank goodness she's not the fussy type.'

'It's all very well, Miss Sara,' Mrs Tennant said indignantly, 'but it's only natural that we should want Mrs Gardner to find everything shipshape. She's had a good holiday, but there's nothing more depressing to my mind than to have to set to as soon as you get back. She'll need a day or two to settle in.'

Dinah and Simon were besides themselves and were busy hatching plans for a welcome of their own, and used to disappear to the bottom of the garden after school.

'I think they're rehearsing some kind of dramatic performance,' Verity told Aunt Emma—one day when she had passed by the summerhouse and heard Dinah's shrill treble declaiming some lines of poetry.

Margot Manley was still calling daily to attend to Aunt Emma, and Garnett had resumed his habit of dropping in at more or less the same time. Verity always found herself some work which necessitated her absence from the room while he was in the house, but she frequently heard the sound of his deep laugh, and could picture the two of them enjoying some joke. Margot never took much notice of Verity, but on the Tuesday after Garnett had left she told Aunt Emma that this was to be her last visit.

Verity had come into the room and heard her say:

' Dr Rhodes is quite satisfied with your progress and I shan't need to come any more. You can use the leg, but try not to do too much at first.'

Aunt Emma thanked her politely; she had admitted that Margot Manley knew her job. As Margot finished packing her equipment Verity took her out to the door and thanked her also for her care of Aunt Emma.

Margot seemed to tower above the younger girl. She had a slightly sarcastic smile on her mouth as she remarked:

' You won't be seeing much of Dr Rhodes now.'

Verity flushed and for a moment felt as if her secret was written all over her face, and then, as the other girl smiled complacently, she realised that indeed her feelings for the doctor were not unknown to the physiotherapist.

' We've always been very great friends since he came to Mardale,' said Margot with seeming irrelevance, but Verity knew that she was being warned off; that Margot wished her to know that Garnett Rhodes was her property.

As she watched the white Austin turn and go down the drive, Verity felt that if it had not been for the delight she felt in contemplating seeing her father and Mary on Thursday, she would have made some excuse to get away for a while. Then, shrugging her shoulders, she went back into the living room.

'Thank goodness she's gone,' Aunt Emma said with relief. 'Oh, I admit she's done her best for me, but I can't stand that big bossy kind of woman.'

Verity was bound to conceal a smile, for Aunt Emma could easily have included herself in the same category, but then she was not the same. Her rather gruff exterior concealed a heart as soft and kind as it was possible to be.

Thursday arrived at last and the house simmered with excitement. Dinah and Simon were busy in the summerhouse, putting the finishing touches to the entertainment they had planned. The house was spick and span and full of flowers. The travellers were expected at about half past three and it seemed an eternity after lunch. Robert had gone into Leeds to meet the train and Laura was with him.

Practically to time Robert's car stopped outside and out of the car stepped Mary, to be engulfed by the children, while Verity, Aunt Emma and the beaming Mrs Tennant waited their turn.

It was almost impossible to imagine how ill John Gardner had been when the tanned smiling man stepped out of the car. Verity could not take her eyes off his face. This strong, happy, healthy person was so far removed from the invalid who had left London Airport nearly three months ago.

Only Sara was missing from the reunion. She had to be on duty, and although she was disappointed she was so used to the discipline of the great hospital that she did not complain, and was looking forward to the evening when she could get home.

When all the greetings were over and things had

calmed down a little, they sat in the large living room and everyone seemed to have so much to say that Verity felt her head spinning. Robert came over to her and whispered:

'I'll have to be off now, Verity. Try to keep Father from coming down to the Works today. If I know him he'll not want to wait until tomorrow.'

'I'll do my best,' she whispered back, and thought she had caught a keen glance from her father as he watched them talk.

After all, it was not difficult to keep John Gardner at home. By the time he had gone round the garden and watched the children's concert it was tea time and nearly time for the Works to close.

'I'll be down first thing in the morning,' he announced. 'I can hardly wait to see how they've been getting on.'

'I'm sure you'll find everything in order,' said Mary with conviction, and her husband agreed with her.

'That lad looks tired all the same,' he said, 'and so does this young lady.'

Verity was sitting on the arm of his chair and not for the first time she gave inward thanks that her father had been spared after his severe illness. She really felt a member of the family now.

Robert telephoned later and after he had spoken to his father he asked if Verity could come to the telephone.

'Can you come down with Father in the morning, Verity? I'd like to get the confession about the loan off my chest as soon as I can. No use putting off the evil moment.'

'Don't worry, Robert, I'll be with him, and I'm sure he'll understand when we explain what happened.'

'I'm not so sure.' Robert sounded despondent. 'You know he really doesn't trust me yet to manage things. I'm still only a boy in his eyes.'

'I think you'll find things will be different now,' Verity tried to reassure him, although she did not look forward to the coming interview with any pleasant anticipation.

The next morning Verity was up early so that she could go with her father to the works. If he was surprised by her desire to accompany him, he made no comment, being so engrossed in his own wish to get there as quickly as possible to see how things were going.

It was touching to see how the workpeople had assembled to welcome him back. It was obvious that he had been greatly missed.

'I'll amuse myself for a while, Robert,' said Verity. 'Father will want to look round and see everything. Just let me know when you want me.'

Her father had not heard this exchange as he was talking to Bill Ellis and so almost without remembering that she was present the two men went off.

There was not much that Verity could see by herself, so at last she went back to the car and sat in it. Her father had left the morning paper and she was engrossed in the crossword when Robert finally came to look for her. He looked a bit pale but resolute and said:

'Come along, better to get it over now when he's in such a good humour at finding that things haven't disintegrated in his absence.'

They went into the office and her father was already back in harness, examining papers, answering the telephone. A good many of his business friends had been eager to get in touch and find out if he was completely recovered.

It was difficult to know how to begin, but Robert took the plunge and told the whole story of the loan, and the circumstances which had led up to his need to ask Verity for help.

Verity watched her father intently but could not read the expression on his face. At one point when he glanced up at his son she fancied she saw the suspicion of a twinkle in his eyes, and then she thought she must have been mistaken.

At last the whole story was told and John Gardner seemed to deliberate for a long time as his son and daughter waited.

'You did very well, my boy,' he said at last and, coming from behind the desk, he gripped Robert's shoulder in a reassuring manner. 'Now go along, I want to talk to Verity about this money we owe to her.'

'You're not annoyed with me?' gasped Robert.

'I'm proud of you both, though I wish you'd told me. I could have helped, but you did what you thought was right and I'm grateful for the fact that you kept all this worry from your mother.'

Robert could not get out of the room quickly enough, his face radiant and the careworn look gone, Verity hoped, for good.

'Now, young lady, we'll have to consider what to do about your money,' said her father. 'What did Mr Everard think about you wanting to keep it all?'

The humour of the situation seemed to strike him and he flung back his head and laughed.

'Daddy!' Verity exclaimed reproachfully. 'It didn't seem funny at the time, and I think I've upset Mr Everard's good opinion of me for ever.'

'Oh, we'll soon put matters right, and I'm going to let you into a secret. Promise, though, that you won't tell Robert.'

'What do you mean?'

'I don't want Robert to know, but if only he'd come to me I could have solved all these difficulties without any of the worry you have both had. Oh,' he continued as Verity was about to speak, 'I'm not at all sorry this happened, it's shown me that I've been completely unfair to Robert, and that in future I owe it to him to let him have a great deal more scope in the running of the firm.'

'How do you mean it could have been avoided?'

'I have always kept a fund for this sort of emergency, but of course, it wouldn't have been available without my signature, and to get that he would have had to tell me. I'm sorry in one way that you've both been so harassed about it, but I'm very proud of my son and daughter.'

'I won't say a word,' Verity promised. 'Robert has done well and it hasn't affected me adversely.' But as she said these words she could not help thinking that all the unpleasantness with Gerard Manley could have been avoided. She had no intention of telling her father about that episode.

Garnett Rhodes came to dinner a few nights later and he was delighted to see the state of John's health, and also that Mary was looking younger and less careworn. Verity was very quiet during the meal. Everyone had been discussing the plans for Sara's wedding and Verity sat with a faraway look. Her abstracted manner did not escape the notice of her father or of Mary, and when they were getting ready for bed that night John wondered aloud:

'There's something wrong with that girl.'

'You mean Verity?'

'Yes. She's obviously a bit depressed about something.'

'Oh, I don't think so. It's probably all this extra work she's been having. Aunt Emma has been telling me how well she managed everything. It's funny considering that when I heard she was coming —I must confess, I had a few doubts about her fitting in.'

'She's part of the family now, that's certain,' said John with satisfaction. 'But I can't help feeling that she's not happy.'

It was late and so no more was said that night, but a few day later Verity received a letter from Mr Everard. She conveyed the contents to her father and Mary.

'It seems there's a little unfinished business to transact and Mr Everard wonders if I could go out to Geneva for a week or two and settle things up. I thought myself it would be a good idea and then I can—' she stopped hastily as she did not want to let out the secret of the money to Mary. Her father understood and it was settled that as soon as her seat on the plane could be booked she would travel out to Geneva.

'The change will do you a world of good,' said Mary.

'It will be lovely to see the Lake and the Everards, and a few old friends, but I don't really want to go away again so soon. Now that I've got to know you all it will be a wrench.'

'Nonsense, it isn't for long, and far better for you to get all the business side finished,' remarked her father. 'I'll get my secretary to make the booking for the plane tomorrow. A holiday out there will put you right.'

'There's nothing wrong with me—really, I'm not at all tired,' she protested.

'Then what is it, my darling? I can tell you're not your usual bright self?'

'Oh!' She gave in. 'Perhaps you're right and I do need a change. It wil be lovely to be in Geneva again, if only on business.'

'Yes, let's get all these formalities out of the way, and then we can settle down to be a complete family at last. Of course Sara wil be getting married—and that reminds me, Mary is set on having a big celebration for your twenty-first birthday. We'll talk about it when you return from Geneva.'

John left for work after a glance at the time and Mary and Verity sat for a while chatting.

'You would tell me, darling, if there was anything really bothering you?' Mary's kind face was concerned.

'Of course I would. I expect I'm a bit tired, but,' she hurried to explain, 'I simply loved looking after things while you were away, and it was quite providential that I got an oportunity to show that I could be of some use. It made such a difference to Sara. It would have taken ages for us to become friends, and now—well, I feel as if I've known her all my life.'

The night before Verity went to Geneva, Garnett Rhodes called once more. It was when John Gardner began to tease Verity a little that his dark face became even more severe.

'You didn't tell us about Mr Everard's nephew Charles,' remarked John.

'What do you mean?' A bright colour suffused Verity's face.

'If I'm not mistaken, that young man is looking forward to seeing you again.'

'Oh, don't be silly, Daddy. Charles and I have known each other since we were so high. He's just a very good friend.'

'That's not the impression he gave me.'

He changed the subject, though, seeing that Verity was embarrassed. Soon after Garnett said a formal goodbye.

'I hope you have a good trip,' he said stiffly.

'Thank you, Doctor—' she began, and then hastily changed it to 'Garnett'. For a moment she thought she saw the suspicion of a twinkle in his eye, but then he was gone and she went up to finish packing.

She had an uneventful flight out and was met at the airport by Charles. He was engaged to one of Verity's friends and she could not help feeling slightly put out by her father's teasing and mention of him when Garnett was around. It did not matter much except that it would perhaps only strengthen his conviction that she was a flirtatious type. Her relationship with Gerard had already done enough damage. She was glad to see Charles again, and made up her mind to enjoy this visit. She walked up through the old part of the town to the University and visited some of her old tutors. Everyone was pleased to welcome her back and she was entertained royally.

Mr Everard did not seem to be in any hurry to bring up the subject of the business which she had come to Geneva to complete. Verity took the long trip by road to Chamonix and revisited the Mer de

Glace. She went up La Grande Salève to the observatory, sending postcards to the children franked at the postbox there.

At last she began to feel that her holiday must come to an end and, curiously, it was at this point that Mr Everard told her that on the following day he would like to see her at his office.

At breakfast there was a letter from Sara and Verity opened it eagerly. It was full of the preparations for the wedding and told all the small details she had longed to hear. It was not until she came to the last page that the blow fell.

'Such a surprise,' wrote Sara. 'Margot Manley was married last Saturday. It was a very hurried affair, but she has known him a long time and I suppose no one was very much surprised in the end.'

Verity sat as if turned to stone. Margot had been very self-confident that day, but against her better judgement Verity had allowed herself to think that perhaps the older girl had been too sure of herself. Now there was no doubt about the fact. She sat for a long time, too hurt for tears, and then she remembered her appointment with Mr Everard, and left the house.

Mrs Everard was concerned. 'Are you all right, my dear? I can easily telephone to my husband and postpone the meeting. You look so pale. I expect you've been out too much in the sunshine.'

'No, no, I'm perfectly well,' Verity protested, and reluctantly Mrs Everard let her go. It was not a long way to the office buildings, but she walked as if in a dream. She felt as if she could not return to Mardale, to see Garnett and Margot happily married, and to be so near to him was almost more than she could bear. She had reached the office now and pulling herself together she went up in the lift to the third floor and after a few minutes the clerk showed her into the office.

Mr Everard seemed in high spirits, and rubbed his hands together in what for him could almost be called a gleeful fashion.

'There are just one or two papers for you to sign,' he said. 'And I've got a very pleasant piece of news for you.'

She listened dumbly, but was suddenly brought to attention by the words which began to penetrate the numbness which had been with her since she read Sara's letter.

'By a very lucky chance,' said Mr Everard, 'your guardian had bought a piece of land by the side of the lake. He had intended to build on it, but after his wife died and he became so ill, the matter was dropped. Now I have great pleasure in telling you that I've sold the plot of land for a very large sum,' and he mentioned an amount which made Verity gasp. 'With this money invested for you, you will be very well provided for, and there will be no need for you to train for any career, unless of course you would wish to do so. I am so glad for you, my dear, dear girl,' and he came over and kissed her on the forehead.

'I wonder,' he went on, 'if your guardian had this in mind. I must admit I was very surprised when his estate was so small, but he was a very shrewd man. We'll never know now.'

Verity was torn between a desire to laugh or to cry. As if it mattered now! A few months ago she would have been overjoyed to be able to help her family without all the anxiety she had gone through, but now it didn't matter. She would go back to

Mardale and continue her studies, and apart from the fact that she would be able to have a car, she felt that her inheritance would make very little difference to her life.

Mr Everard was looking a trifle surprised at the lack of any enthusiasm on the part of his client.

'I am glad, of course, Mr Everard,' she said finally. 'And it's good of you to take so much trouble about my affairs.'

The old man had to be satisfied with this lukewarm reception of his news, and as there was nothing else to discuss she made her way to the lake, and sat for a long time watching the *mouettes* and steamers. She rose at last and went over the bridge to the shops and spent a comparatively happy hour or two buying gifts for all the family. This time she had no need for economy and for a little while she forgot her heartache as she carefully selected things likely to please all of them, and took particular pleasure in those chosen for the two small children.

'You don't seem to be very happy.' This was Charles at the party his uncle gave to announce his nephew's engagement to Thérèse Monfort.

'Are you sure it wasn't a mistake to go to Yorkshire and try to pick up the threads of family life?' he asked in some concern, for Verity, although outwardly bright and enjoying herself, had been his friend for too long for him to be deceived.

'It's not the family, Charles,' she answered.

'Some man?' he guessed, and she nodded.

'Is it someone who's let you down?'

In an instant the golden eyes flamed,

'It's not his fault at all, only mine for being so foolish. He was already promised to another girl before I ever met him. No, Charles,' she continued,

'I've just got to go back and face up to things, but it's going to be difficult to live in the same village, to meet his wife.'

'You don't care for her?'

'How did you guess?' She laughed at last, at her own foolishness, and said:

'No more looking back. I'll be all right Charles, truly. You can't have any idea how much it means to me to have a home and family in England. When I was left, as I thought, without a relative in the world it seemed like a miracle that I should have a real father and brothers and sisters.'

Charles said no more, but she was conscious of his sympathy, and was able to rejoice in his happiness.

It seemed an interminable time before all the business formalities about the piece of land were concluded and Verity began to long for home again. At last all the documents were signed and her inheritance safely invested to bring in a very handsome monthly income. Mr Everard was almost purring with delight. It had offended his sense of what was right that the girl he had known from childhood should have to lower her standard of living. He was unaware that to Verity this aspect of the situation had never been of any account.

'Thank you for all you've done for me,' she said to the elderly lawyer. 'And now I must get back to Mardale. I know you'll understand, but I've seen so little of my father yet that I'm impatient to be back. It has been a wonderful holiday here with you and Mrs Everard, and I'm feeling so very much better for the change of scene.'

He did not try to press her to stay, and her flight home was booked. She spent the last few days with her friends. This would always be her second home and she toyed with the idea of keeping the flat which was at present let. Mr Everard had been going to sell it for her, but she felt that it would be ideal for the family to be able to use it for holidays, and now she could afford to pay for it to be kept in order.

As she stood once more at the airport at Geneva memories of that last occasion flooded back into her mind. How she had looked forward, half dreading, but with excitement, to her meeting with her father, her arrival at London Airport, and the wait in the restaurant and then that first unforgettable meeting with Garnett Rhodes. She could not fight back the tears, and Mr Everard was concerned.

'It's nothing,' she protested. 'You've been so kind to me and I can't help remembering how forlorn I felt the last time we stood here. It's different now. I have a place in the world and a home and family who are not any longer unfamiliar, shadowy figures.'

Once more she said goodbye as her flight was called and she flew out of Geneva in the morning sunlight. She was going home and she was happy about this, but in the secret recesses of her heart there was an ache which could not be assuaged.

CHAPTER VIII

'Well, I'll be—' John Gardner gave a low whistle of surprise.

'What is it?' Mary looked up from her own correspondence to see her husband staring at the letter in his hand with an expression she could not interpret.

He passed over the letter and she saw that it was from Verity, and as she read it she understood the reason for his exclamation.

'Old Everard made some very mysterious remarks when we were out there, but I had no idea that this windfall was going to turn up for Verity. I'd got used to the idea that she wasn't after all an heiress and in fact—' he paused.

'You're not really too pleased about it, are you? said Mary.

'I don't know. I always feel it's better to earn one's way in life. I only hope that it won't spoil Verity.'

'No need to worry about that. She's not capable of becoming spoilt. My guess is that she'll be so busy giving all the money away, she'll never think of herself.'

'She says she's returning on the next possible flight, so I suppose we can expect her any time now.'

'I shall be very glad to have her back. I had no idea I could become so fond of anyone in such a short time. I do hope the holiday has done her good. There was some worry on her mind when she went away, I'm sure of that.'

'I must be off,' said John, kissing his wife and

making for the door. 'Don't say anything about this money to anyone until she's actually here. I suppose we shall have to let it leak out then. I don't think it will make any difference now to the others. They've learned to love her for herself.'

Mary went upstairs to see to Verity's room, and as she stood by the dressing table looking at the picture of the two people who had taken charge of the girl from her babyhood, she said in her heart a silent 'thank you' for the way in which they had carried out the task, and thanked heaven, not for the first time, that her relationship with her stepdaughter was such a good one. Her own position, first as the new mother to the two older children, had been trying enough. She had dreaded, more than she had ever revealed to her husband, the arrival of this stranger. Now all her doubts were resolved and the whole family united.

Later in the morning a telegram arrived from Verity announcing that she would be arriving the following day. It said 'Expect me Tuesday, 28th. Will make my own way home.'

Mary felt slightly put out that she could not arrange to have the girl met as she did not know which train she would be catching from King's Cross, but then she realised that Verity was quite able to take care of herself and would prefer no fussing.

Preparations were well under way for Sara's wedding in the middle of October, and as Verity was to be one of the bridesmaids it was a good thing she was returning in time for the dress fittings. Indeed, she would be a great help, Mary felt sure, in keeping the two children out of mischief. Then, when all the bustle of the wedding was over, Mary was determined to arrange some kind of celebration for Verity

—not only because she had missed all the fun of a twenty-first party but because it would be a good way of introducing her to the neighbourhood.

On the morning of the twenty-eighth Garnett Rhodes called to see Aunt Emma. This lady was now fully recovered, but it had been decided she must stay until after Sara's wedding, and Garnett's visit was by way of being a final one to check that the injured leg was fully recovered.

After he had seen his patient, Mary persuaded him to stay for coffee and he seemed glad to rest for a while. Mary thought he had a tired and somewhat strained look. She chattered on inconsequently, and it was only when she mentioned that Verity was about to return that he stiffened, and an expression hard to read came over his face. Mary was excited and perhaps she told him more than her husband would have approved. One of the things which she revealed was that when Verity had first come to Mardale she had not been the wealthy young person that everyone had imagined. She told something of the way in which the girl had helped them all and Garnett's expression grew more inscrutable.

After he had gone Mary wondered guiltily if she had revealed more that she should have done, but she consoled herself that at least she had kept quiet about the fact that the myth about Verity's inheritance had now turned to reality.

Garnett wore a very thoughtful expression as he drove away, but he had little time for thinking about Mary's disclosures as he found a rush of work waiting for him when he returned to the surgery. During the afternoon he had to go into Leeds to the big hospital and to visit one or two patients who were receiving treatment there. He spent a busy afternoon, and it was just as he was about to leave and was saying goodbye to one of the consultant surgeons that the alarm came in. In a minute the huge place was a hive of activity, and Garnett asked what was going on.

Ambulances were leaving the forecourt as quickly as they could be staffed, and when he learned that there had been a bad railway accident reported just outside Leeds he asked if his services would be of any use, and his offer was gratefully accepted. It was a bad time for the call as it was one of the operating days and many of the staff were tied up in the theatre.

He decided to go in his own car and followed closely the ambulance as it left with bells ringing and lights flashing.

It was about half past six and still daylight, and as they sped along the road the traffic gave way to the convoy of police and hospital vehicles, he hoped and prayed that the casualties would not be too heavy. He was glad he had been in Leeds and would be able to give a helping hand to his overworked colleagues.

As the procession of vehicles came to halt and he got his first glimpse of the terrible pile of wreckage strewn along the line, his heart sank. It seemed impossible that anyone could remain alive in such a scene of destruction. A strange silence brooded over the scene, broken only by the voices of the helpers who seemed to be talking in whispers. Two of the long coaches had come off the rails, fortunately just before the train had reached a deep cutting. A few yards further and they would have fallen down the embankment.

The door of the ambulance directly in front of him

opened and the team of doctors and nurses clambered out, and among them was Sara. She was a very efficient nurse, as he well knew, and he was amazed to see that her usual calm seemed to have deserted her, and as she saw him she gave a cry and ran to his side. He was getting his bag out of the car and then he turned to her. He was about to tell her sharply to pull herself together when she stammered:

'Garnett, Verity might be on this train!'

'What do you mean?' His hands grasped her shoulders and she cried out in pain.

'Do you know what train this is?' she pleaded.

'I hadn't time to find out, tell me what makes you think—' He was unable to continue. Then the instincts of his profession came to his aid and taking the girl by the hand he said:

'Come along, whatever train this is, these people are in need of our help. Tell me what you know as we work.'

And as they started to climb up the embankment she gasped out her story.

'I had a letter from Verity this morning and she told me that she would be returning from King's Cross this afternoon. I was just on my way to telephone home when the call came in for an emergency. I was going off duty for the day.'

'Can you come this way, sir?' a man's voice called, and for the next hour or so he had no time to pause for thought. Only the calls on his professional skill kept him from giving way to the desire to run up and down the length of the piled-up wreckage, from calling her name desperately. He looked at his strong skilful hands and longed to be with the men who toiled ceaselessly, themselves often in danger among the splintered woodwork and steel which reared in grotesque fashion. He looked at each person as they treated them and prayed silently that she had not been on this train; that she would be travelling on a later one, and that all their fears would prove to be groundless.

It became evident that many people had only minor injuries. The number of those in a serious condition was small and so far there had been no report of any deaths, but there was still the farther coach to search. Both he and Sara were almost unrecognisable by now. They were covered with grime, but they continued to work steadily, neither speaking much. It seemed as if they had thrust from their thoughts the one thing which should have been uppermost in their minds, and Sara had regained her composure.

It was as they reached the last carriage and stood aside to let stretcher-bearers pass that he saw her.

Beside the wreckage, the litter of broken glass, she crouched, holding in her arms a baby. Her fair hair concealed her face from him, but it was unmistakably Verity. Sara recognised her almost at the same moment and with a cry she rushed forward and touched her sister on the shoulder. The girl turned, but her whole being seemed to be concentrated on some other problem and she looked at them in a dazed unrecognising way.

' The mother,' she gasped. ' She's underneath the coach. I can hear her calling!'

And as they listened they too could hear the faint voice crying.

The rescue team tore at the sides of the carriage. It seemed an eternity until at last, slowly and painfully, they dragged the woman clear. Sara had taken the baby from her sister, who had sunk down on the grass beside the track, unable to stand.

Garnett made a swift examination of the now unconscious woman, quite young, dark-haired and slender. Verity cried out in alarm:

'She can't—' and quickly Garnett came to her side.

'She'll be all right, Verity, I promise you. She's suffering from slight concussion and of course shock, but in a day or two she'll be as fit as ever.'

The rescuers had established that there were no more passengers on the train and, carrying the baby, Sara led the way to the ambulance. Garnett helped Verity and felt such a tremendous relief that he could hardly refrain from clasping her in his arms. However, once more his professional judgement came to his aid and he insisted that she be taken with the mother and baby to the hospital for a complete check-up.

There was plenty of work to occupy him at the hospital, but at Sara's request he managed to get a message through to John Gardner at Mardale to say that Verity was safe. Though Sara had not managed to get the message through about Verity being on the train, the family had been extremely anxious as they had known that she would have reached England, and they were greatly relieved to get his news.

'Are you sure she's not hurt, Garnett?' This was Mary, who had taken over the receiver.

'I'm quite sure, but I thought it best for her to have a check before she comes home. Don't worry, Mary, I'll see she gets to you as soon as possible. I don't know about Sara, she might have to remain on duty.'

By the time Verity came out from the casualty department, tidy now, but pale and with a dark bruise on her cheek, Garnett had finished all he could do to help and was ready to take her home.

Verity was worried about the baby, but on finding her safely ensconced in the children's ward, and quite unharmed, she was ready to leave, and as Garnett expected, Sara had volunteered to stay on to relieve the overworked casualty department.

Verity leaned back against the comfortable seat with a sigh of relief and then she began to talk. Garnett made no attempt to stop her as he knew that this was the best way of getting the shock out of her system. She told him how she had been alone in the last carriage with the girl and the baby. They had got friendly as women do and just before the accident happened Verity had offered to nurse the child while the other girl took down her case from the rack. It was just as she was reaching up for it that the train began to rock and sway and then came the appalling crash. Verity did not know how she came to be beside the train outside the carriage, but as she was near the door it probably opened and she was flung out. The other girl was trapped.

Garnett felt that he would be glad to get her home and he travelled as quickly as he dared. It was time she was put to bed with a sedative, and as soon as he got her safely to the house and into Mary's care, he left some tablets and instructions and went away.

Verity slept until nearly lunch time next day. Dr Elliot called, but did not disturb her. Sara had arrived home for a much needed rest and was also in bed. As Mary prepared the lunch she rejoiced for the blessed fact that all her brood were safe, and suppressed a shudder as she remembered how nearly Verity's journey home had ended in tragedy.

At last she heard sounds of the girl moving and went up to see how her stepdaughter was feeling now. In spite of the dark bruise which stood out against the fair skin, she looked refreshed, but her face still had that wistful unfulfilled expression which had puzzled Mary before Verity had gone to Geneva. They did not talk much about the crash. After Verity had satisfied herself that the baby and her mother were safe and recovering, she went on to talk of her time in Geneva, and purposely she avoided any mention of Dr Rhodes. There were a thousand questions about his marriage to Margot which she half longed yet half dreaded to ask. She did not want to arouse any suspicion in the minds of her family that she regarded him in anything but the light of a friend.

Mary finally finished telling her all the family news, and about the preparations in hand for Sara's wedding.

'When you're feeling better we must get on with the fittings for your dress,' she said, and at this moment Sara came into the room and they talked about the plans which were up to the moment going smoothly enough.

That night Verity had a long talk with her father about her unexpected inheritance and managed to persuade him, for he was reluctant to touch any of her capital, to allow her to invest a quite considerable sum in the business. It would help him to expand as he had wanted to do for a long time, and ease the worries which attend the running of a small family firm on a small amount of capital.

It was just as they had finished their talk that Robert arrived and just after him came Garnett Rhodes. John Gardner took Robert into his study to tell him the news about the firm's future prospects, so Verity was left alone with the doctor.

There was a certain feeling of stiffness apparent between them. The conversation touched only upon questions about her health and whether she had recovered from the shock of yesterday's events.

Then Verity ventured shyly:

'I haven't had time to offer you my congratulations yet, Garnett. I only heard the news just before I left Geneva.'

He looked slightly surprised, but answered coolly enough.

'Oh, it's nothing, I've only just got the results myself and didn't know that anyone had heard about it.'

There was another uneasy silence and then they both started to speak at the same time.

'I meant your marriage—' began Verity.

'I must congratulate you too on your engagement—' said Garnett. Then the silence deepened until the tension between them became almost unbearable.

Suddenly Garnett rose and came over to where she sat by the window, her face still pale and the mark on her cheek dark and swollen against the fragile skin. He seemed to tower above her and she shrank back a little. For some reason this seemed to anger him.

'Why do you always shrink away from me?' The words burst forth. 'And what on earth do you mean "my marriage"? Nothing is farther from my thoughts, unless—'

'Why,' she stammered, 'Sara wrote to tell me about Margot's marriage, and naturally I thought she'd married you.'

He stared at her in stunned amazement.

'How on earth could you have got such an idea?'

he questioned, and then suddenly the dark face lost its frown, the white teeth flashed and he threw back his head and laughed and laughed as if he would never stop.

'But Margot almost—' she stopped, not wanting to be disloyal to the other girl.

He sighed a little.

'I'm afraid Margot got caught up in a dream in which there was no foundation of fact, and I expect at this moment she's thanking her stars she had such a lucky escape. Margot never loved me. When James Carver arrived back from his research Fellowship in the States, she never had any more time for me. It was a big misunderstanding. James was too shy to ask her to wait for him, but now all is well and they're by now on their way back to America. He's to take up a post there next month.'

'But why did Ger—' She stopped again as his face once more assumed that grim look.

'So that's why you went out with that young blackguard!' and he muttered a few words which boded ill for Gerard if ever their paths should cross.

'Verity,' he began carefully, 'tell me one thing before we run into any more misunderstandings. Are you engaged to that fellow Charles?'

He shot out the words so vehemently that Verity almost smiled, and then as she gave a decided negative to his question she found herself swept up into an embrace which seemed as if it would never end. He held her close and she felt that same sense of security which she had never thought to find again. He stroked back the shining hair and kissed the bruised cheek gently before his kisses became more urgent, and she responded with a joy she had thought impossible to achieve.

At last they drew apart.

'What a lot of time we've wasted—' he began, but she put her finger upon his lips.

'No, not wasted. I wouldn't have missed a moment of it.'

Perhaps she deceived herself, but all the fears, and anxieties, seemed to have vanished, and only the knowledge of their mutual love and trust remained.

The door opened, but they did not hear it until an injured voice proclaimed to the world at large:

'Why is Dr Rhodes kissing Verity?' and in a moment the room seemed to be full.

John Gardner wore a slightly bemused air, but he rallied manfully from the shock of discovering that the daughter he had only just regained was shortly to leave him. Mary was delighted and was heard to murmur that she must find Aunt Emma and tell her the news as that lady wouldn't be in the least surprised.

'What do you mean?' cried Verity.

'Oh, she spotted what was wrong with you and told me before you came home. She said everything would turn out well for you in the long run.'

'Let me get over the wedding of my eldest daughter before you start making any plans to deprive me of the second,' begged John.

'Don't make us wait too long, sir.'

Garnett was holding Verity to him as if he would like to bear her off with him at that moment. Then looking down at her he said:

'I think she's had enough excitement for today. She had a bad shock yesterday.' And under his breath he murmured, 'And so did I.'

It was not until a few weeks later at the reception for

Sara when Verity, radiant in her bridesmaid's dress, had deserted the best man and gone to Garnett's side that she gave the secret of her inheritance away. It was an unguarded word on her part which made him take her by the shoulders and ask sternly:

'What do you mean? Your inheritance?'

She pulled him from the reception room, into a little sitting room at the side. Then she started to laugh.

'Don't be cross, Garnett, but I am an heiress after all.' Swiftly she told him about the unexpected turn of events which had taken her out to Geneva. She explained how she was using the money to help her family, and although at first he was not too pleased to find that he was not to be her sole means of support, finally he laughed too and said as he gathered her in his arms:

'What does it matter? We belong together, neither money or any other matter shall ever come between us, my darling,' and as she lifted her lips for his kiss she felt that she had come home and was no longer a stranger at the door.